WILD HEART

KINGDOM OF WOLVES

C.R. JANE
MILA YOUNG

CONTENTS

JOIN OUR READERS' GROUP

Stay up to date with C.R. Jane by joining her Facebook readers' group, C.R.'s Fated Realm. Ask questions, get first looks at new books/series, and have fun with other book lovers!

Join C.R. Jane's Group

www.facebook.com/groups/C.R.FatedRealm

❧

Join Mila Young's Wicked Readers Group to chat directly with Mila and other readers about her books, enter giveaways, and generally just have loads of fun!

Join Mila Young's Group

www.facebook.com/groups/milayoungwickedreaders

KINGDOM OF WOLVES SERIES

FROM C.R. JANE AND MILA YOUNG

Wild Moon
Wild Heart
Wild Girl

These stories are set in the Kingdom of Wolves shared world, but our series will follow Rune's continuing story with her alphas.

WILD HEART

REAL WOLVES BITE...

I ran from my fated mate.

I drove to the middle of nowhere, where I thought I'd be safe.

And somehow, I ended up here.

Amarok has secrets. And it's a town filled with shifters.

The very thing I've been trying to get away from.

My arrival has shattered the fragile peace this town's had for the last century.

War is coming between the two packs, and only I seem to have the ability to stop it.

The two alphas in the town are determined to have me.

But a killer wants the very same thing.

Me? I just want whatever's inside of me to be released.

Like Wilder and Daxon, I carry my own secrets, ones that make it impossible for my fated mate to let me go.

They call me wild...

But I just want to be free.

1

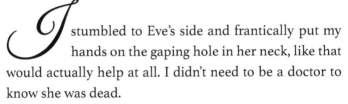 stumbled to Eve's side and frantically put my hands on the gaping hole in her neck, like that would actually help at all. I didn't need to be a doctor to know she was dead.

I screamed for help, not letting up until my voice was hoarse. Where the fuck was everyone? It looked like something had torn a huge chunk out of her neck. Blood was still pouring out of the wound, meaning this was a recent kill. It coated the ground at my feet and was all over my hands. What kind of creature could have done that? It was certainly not like any wolf bite I'd seen, that was for sure.

I opened my mouth to scream again, but just then, a branch cracked from somewhere in the woods behind me. Shivers shot up my spine as I heard the sound of someone breathing heavily. I'd stumbled into something right out of a horror movie. I swung around, not wanting to be jumped from behind, but I didn't immediately see anything out of the ordinary besides the swaying branches of the trees and shrubs as an unusually cold wind ripped through the forest.

More branches broke, and a giant shadow busted through the underbrush, coming close enough that I could make out its existence while still staying sheltered by the trees and away from the path. It really was some kind of shadow creature. I was unable to make anything out besides the fact that it was freaking enormous and had eyes that seemed like they were glowing.

I stumbled backwards, my bloody hands outstretched as my heart beat out of my chest. *Fuck*, why did I have to be so worthless with my own wolf?

A low growl sounded out from the monster. It reverberated around me, digging into my skin and sending dread spasming through my stomach. An itching sensation began to spread through my limbs, so intense, I was fighting back the urge to start scratching at my skin, even as I prepared myself to be attacked.

Something pulsed in my gut, once, twice, and then a third time. It felt like something was stabbing me from the inside. The sensation was so intense and strange, I fell backwards onto the path, the loose stones on the ground digging and cutting into my skin.

The shadow creature let out a sharp whine and disappeared into thin air. He hadn't just moved deeper into the forest, he'd literally just vanished. There one second and then gone the next.

The pulsing sensation had stopped, but my body was shaking from the adrenaline rush of avoiding certain death. My breath was coming out in gasps as I became aware of the rest of my surroundings once again. Like the blood touching my fingertips and the sound of yells and running footsteps approaching from somewhere farther up the path.

I scrambled up to my feet, hoping this was someone who could help and not something else. The path curved up ahead, and I jumped when a snarling grey wolf sped towards me, his mouth curled in a growl. A few people that I only faintly recognized from seeing them in town appeared next. They all halted in place when they saw me standing over Eve's body. The wolf prowled forward and growled once again.

I belatedly realized what I looked like, standing there, covered in blood right next to Eve's corpse.

I held up my hands beseechingly. "I just found her. I've been calling for help," I cried. "I was bringing the catering." I pointed to the dropped tray of food like an idiot, hoping it could convince them of my innocence.

One of the guys barked something at the wolf who was inching closer, and it stopped moving. The guy ran to the side of Eve and checked her pulse. "She's dead," he told the others, who all had various looks of grief written across their features.

"No," one of the women gasped. She buried her head in the shoulder of the other man, a middle-aged guy wearing an oversized flannel with salt and pepper flecked hair. He glared at me, the pupils of his eyes expanding menacingly like I'd somehow become enemy number one.

"You're the new girl in town, aren't you?" he said roughly.

I swallowed and took a step back, sensing that the

threat of danger wasn't past. The man who'd been examining Eve stood up, his face pained. His eyes snapped to mine, and I watched as his eyes changed. His hands extended into long claws.

"Please, I didn't have anything to do with this," I whispered.

He snarled, his eyes wild. He'd obviously lost control of his wolf. I knew from experience in my old pack that it was all downhill when that happened.

A snarl ripped through the air, and suddenly, Wilder was in front of me, his teeth bared. As a Lycan wolf, he could only change on the full moon, unlike the Bitten wolf who'd been about to jump me, but Wilder was very much still a force to be reckoned with. You could feel his power reverberating through the air. The man who'd lost control immediately dropped his gaze and bared his throat, falling to his knees in front of us. Wilder advanced on him stealthily, snarling one more time for good measure. The other two people had also fallen to their knees and were looking down, throats bared. It took me a second to realize I should have had the urge to do the same, as I'd always done it in the past. Looking back, I'd done it with Wilder and Daxon at times since I'd been here.

The fact that I wasn't feeling a pull to do it now was certainly an interesting development. I heard the snarl of a motorcycle from far away, and within what seemed like seconds, Daxon was suddenly there, intercepting Wilder's advance on the other Bitten wolf.

"What do you think you're doing?" Daxon snarled at Wilder. I watched, mesmerized, as his eyes shifted back and forth from human to wolf. He was trying to control himself, and I hoped for everyone's sake he would succeed. Neither Wilder nor Daxon seemed to have noticed the pressing issue of Eve. My heart squeezed in my chest as my gaze flicked back to Eve's lifeless form. She was staring up at the sky, wide-eyed. She almost looked shocked. I hoped for her sake the attack had been unexpected and quick.

Daxon and Wilder were still having some sort of bull-shit standoff, and the three other townspeople were eyeing each other nervously, like they were preparing to run if things got serious.

"Losing control of your people, Dax?" Wilder asked sarcastically.

Daxon threw a disdainful look at the three quivering people still kneeling on the ground. "I can handle my own," he said through gritted teeth.

"Then why was Conley about to attack Rune?" asked Wilder, pointing a rigid finger at the man in question.

Daxon's face went blank. His golden gaze turned cold, spine-chilling actually. I'd never seen him look like that. His eyes were usually warm, caring, sweet...with the exception of when he'd stalked me through the woods. The man in front of me was a stranger. There was some-thing playing in his gaze, a hint of madness almost, that had my stomach churning with a mixture of fear...and lust.

I probably needed to talk to a therapist about that.

Daxon's gaze flicked to mine briefly and softened as he examined me, as if he was making sure I was all right.

I didn't know how he could tell either way. I was covered in blood.

Whatever he saw must have been enough to reassure him that I wasn't about to keel over because Daxon's face transformed back into the scary, deadly stranger from before as he turned to face Conley. Daxon stalked towards him like he was prey. Conley was a sniveling, shivering mess at that point. Daxon squatted down in front of him, his nails on his right hand transforming into sharp black-tipped claws, much longer than the ones Conley had displayed. I watched in horror-struck fascination as Daxon gripped Conley's jaw, tiny rivulets of blood dropping from Conley's face as he did so.

"Were you going to attack Rune?" Daxon purred in what might have been the scariest voice I'd ever heard. The front of Conley's pants darkened as he wet himself in stark fear of whatever Daxon was about to do.

Wilder snorted at the sight, and then the woman let out a pitiful cry. That was enough to jerk me back to my senses.

"Daxon," I snapped, weaving around Wilder's body and rushing towards him. "Haven't you noticed that Eve's dead?" My voice caught on a cry as I pulled his clawed hand away from Conley's face.

Daxon used his other arm to throw Conley down to the ground before standing up. I could feel Wilder's warmth as he crowded me in from behind.

I resisted the urge to scoot back into Wilder's embrace while pulling Daxon with me. Despite the fact that I was still furious at Daxon, still furious at both of them really, I found myself craving both of their touches.

It's just because of the situation, I told myself, unable to admit anything else...even in my own head.

I jerked my hand away from Daxon, and in a blink, he was next to Eve's body. With a gentleness that surprised me, he softly stroked Eve's cheek and closed her eyes. He then sprung up and let out the most mournful howl I'd ever heard. It was the sound of pure heartbreak. The three others echoed his howls, and then I heard more sound in the distance where I assumed a large crowd of people were gathered for the picnic. A tear slid down my cheek as more people appeared around the corner, pure devastation present in all of them.

Daxon's howls quieted, and his whole body quivered. I heard him let out a long exhale like he was trying to get a hold of himself. As the crowd grew, just a few feet away from me, their murmurs grew louder. Their eyes flicked from Eve to my blood-covered form, accusations in their eyes that were hard to bear.

Another loud cry ripped through the crowd, the sound somehow filled with even more pain than the others I'd heard. A woman pushed her way through the crowd, her eyes the same color and shape as Eve's. She let out an inhuman wail as she collapsed to Eve's side, burying her face in Eve's chest as giant sobs wracked her body.

She must have been Eve's mother. Shame that I shouldn't have felt coursed through me. It was like everyone's accusations and assumptions were sinking into me...making me feel like I'd somehow done something wrong.

Daxon snapped his finger at one of the men in the

crowd, and he came and comforted the weeping, raging woman as Daxon turned his attention back to me.

"Rune," he said softly, the words heavy in the air. I let out a hiccuped sob.

"I was just coming to deliver the food," I whispered, half-heartedly gesturing to somewhere behind me where the tray of steak bites was still strewn across the path. Wilder had now stepped up right behind me until his body was practically cradling mine. I shivered despite his warmth. "She was lying here, already dead." I took a deep breath, trying to get ahold of myself. "There was something in the woods, a creature. I'd never seen anything like it. It was right over there," I explained, pointing to where the shadow thing had been.

Wilder moved away from me in an instant, stalking his way towards where I'd pointed. I wondered how long it was going to take for me to get used to how fast he and Daxon moved. No one in my old pack, including Alistair, had shown that kind of speed. Wilder sniffed the air and crinkled up his nose in disgust. "It smells like sulfur and smoke," he commented as he moved deeper into the woods. My stomach rolled in worry as I watched him, sure that the shadow thing was going to make an appearance at any moment. Daxon hadn't moved from in front of me. He was watching the crowd with hard eyes, as if he was daring them to keep talking about me. I probably should have sent him after Wilder, who'd just disappeared from sight, but I had a sinking suspicion that Daxon's presence was the only thing keeping the crowd from coming at me. "Is that Eve's mother?" I asked softly, resisting the urge to go to the woman and comfort her. That obviously wouldn't go over well.

"Yes," Daxon whispered just as softly. "She was her only child. They'd been having trouble lately, fighting more and more. I guess Eve had been acting strange." He sighed and ran an anxious hand through his tousled golden locks. "Lydia's never going to recover from this."

I thought of Eve's secret relationship with Daniel. I was sure it was behind Eve's strange behavior.

Daniel. My heart thudded with the reminder that he still had to find out about this. He'd been crazy about Eve. I could tell. What was this going to do to him?

Wilder appeared from behind a tree, and I let out a sigh of relief. He shook his head at Daxon, answering an unspoken question.

"You did this," Eve's mother suddenly screamed. Her nails sharped into short, ferociously sharp claws as she lunged towards me. Daxon caught her before she could reach me, and she began to beat against his chest, snarling to get to me.

"Calm," Daxon ordered, Alpha power threaded through his words as he spoke. She collapsed against him, her fight completely gone as she wept into his shirt. The blood she'd gotten on her while embracing Eve's body stained Daxon's white button-up. The whole scene was utterly heartbreaking.

Wilder reached an arm around my waist, and Daxon snarled. "Don't touch her," he seethed, his eyes flashing.

Watching his eyes...and everything else that I'd seen just now, reminded me what an idiot I'd been to ignore all the blatant signs in front of me that Wilder and

Daxon, and the rest of this town, were so much more than human. It was amazing what the mind could do when it wanted to protect itself.

Daxon looked torn between wanting to rip Wilder's hand off of me and continue to comfort his pack member, who was still sobbing in his arms. The woman in question lifted her head from Daxon's shirt and shot me a furious glare filled with so much hate that I could practically taste it.

"I'm getting her away from this mess. You need to handle the situation," Wilder growled out, and I sighed in frustration that even in the midst of this crisis, they were still doing their alpha a-hole competitive thing.

"I have the inn's catering van," I murmured softly, my gaze dancing to various members of Daxon's pack that all looked like they were seconds away from going against their alpha and trying to kill me. If they thought about it, the idea that I was capable of killing Eve was ludicrous. She'd had the ability to harness her wolf powers. I was as weak as a lamb. Certainly not a threat to anyone.

People always feared the unknown though. It was much easier to blame something on someone they could see instead of acknowledging the fact that there was a monster prowling the woods around their town.

"You're not going anywhere alone," Wilder snarled, plastering me to his hard body. His touch felt almost desperate...like he was afraid I was just going to disappear.

Looking at all the townspeople currently glaring my way, it seemed like it just might be a good idea to disappear.

Daxon looked torn between wanting to be with me or fight Wilder, I couldn't be sure...and being there for his people.

"We can drive in the van," I said firmly, a wave of exhaustion hitting me. It had been an eventful twenty-four hours, and tonight, seeing Eve like that...I wasn't going to get over it any time soon.

Daxon pushed the crying woman into another pack member's arms and then grabbed my hand and pulled me away from Wilder until I was flush against his body. He stroked my cheek while he stared into my eyes. "Everything's going to be all right, baby," he whispered, his tone and touch at odds with the intense look in his eye.

I wished I could have believed him, but I'd learned early on that nothing was ever all right in my life. Even when everything seemed to be good, there was always something waiting just around the corner to ruin everything.

I just hadn't imagined that the thing lurking around the corner was a terrifying shadow monster.

Daxon reluctantly let me go and then started barking orders. Wilder grabbed my hand and started to pull me the opposite direction down the path. As I walked away from the group, I saw that they were gathering Eve's body and heading in the direction of where the party had been taking place. A few of the women were leading Eve's mother's trembling body behind the somber procession.

A sob tore at my throat, and I hurried away from the sight. Wilder took the keys from me when we reached the van. The back doors of it were still open from where I'd left them, thinking I'd be right back to grab more food. I tiredly watched as Wilder slammed them closed and then walked me to the passenger side of the van. I felt like a zombie, like I was just a stranger in someone else's body that was just going through the movements. I got into the seat, and Wilder buckled my seatbelt before shutting the door and going around to the driver's side. He got in and started the van and then wordlessly drove us back to the inn.

We pulled up to the back of the inn, Wilder obviously being familiar with how the catering worked at the place. Jim came out with a worried look on his face, his arms crossed in front of him as he watched us questioningly. I just sat there in the van, unmoving, staring blankly at some plaster that needed to be repaired near one of the large windows back there.

"Sweetheart," Wilder said softly, and a little cry burst from my lips at how out of place the tender words seemed in the situation. Wilder sighed and then got out of the van. I watched as he said something to Jim and Jim's face collapsed in sorrow. He must have told him about Eve.

I'd obviously not known Eve terribly well, but it would have been obvious to anyone that she was the kind of person the world would miss. She just had this light about her that you didn't see in very many people.

My door suddenly opened, and I realized I'd gotten lost in my head again. I lamely protested when Wilder unbuckled my seatbelt and then scooped me up in his arms. He carried me through the back door next to a grieving Jim, who was now talking to Carrie, all the way up the stairs to my room.

"We need to do something about this," Wilder muttered as he sat me down on the bed. He briefly disappeared from the room, and I heard the sound of water.

He was running me a freaking bath.

Things between me and him were complicated. And there was the matter of Daxon.

But did I let him lead me into the bathroom? Did I let him strip me down? Did I let him gently run a warm washcloth over my skin, touching me like he was worshiping me rather than washing me? Yep.

Just like the sweet way he'd spoken to me in the van earlier, the soft way he was touching me in the bathtub... it just did something to me. It broke something inside me. I was so starved for affection and care that it was like my body didn't know what to do with it when it got it.

Wilder was kneeling down next to the tub and only looked mildly alarmed as I randomly burst into tears and buried my face in my hands. He didn't say anything, and I needed it that way. I needed to sit in the silence with him and mourn that things really sucked.

After yet another breakdown, I got into bed, exhausted. Wilder turned to go, and I patted the space next to me. "Lie with me?" I asked hoarsely. My body was shutting down, something it tended to do under extreme stress, and today had certainly been one for the books.

Wilder looked relieved and carefully lay down next to me without taking any of his clothes off. I buried my face into his neck and breathed in his scent. His chest rumbled against me in a soft purr, and I soaked the comforting sound in.

"Goodnight, Rune," he whispered in a gravelly, tired voice.

"Goodnight," I whispered back.

I still had nightmares that night, but I somehow knew his presence was preventing them from being worse.

Wilder was gone when I opened my eyes the next morning.

*M*y stomach heaved each time I thought of Eve in the woods. I didn't want to remember her that way, but it was funny how my brain insisted on reminding me of all the things I didn't want to see. Like her dead eyes staring up into the sky. When I glanced down at my hands, I pictured them covered in her blood and how much I would have done anything to save her if I had found her in time.

I moved into the bathroom and turned on the water in the sink and lathered my hands with the soap. I rubbed them into a white mass, then used my toothbrush to scrub under my nails again. I had to get rid of this horrible feeling like I couldn't wash her death off me.

"You did nothing wrong," I murmured under my breath and lifted my chin to catch my gaze in the mirror. I looked startled. It was the best way to describe the paleness of my cheeks, the red puffiness of my eyes from crying for the past half hour since waking up. I barely knew her, but we'd worked together at Moonstruck Diner enough times to make her loss hurt.

Lowering my head, not wanting to look at myself a second longer, I washed my hands, dried them on the towel, and staggered into the main room. There, I peered out the window to the grounds below. The river glistened beneath the sun, but it had no right looking so beautiful and calm after someone so young lost their life.

My throat squeezed, and I blinked away more tears.

Down by the woods, locals gathered, and I wouldn't be surprised if they suddenly appeared in front of the inn with pitchforks and fire, demanding my death.

I might have laughed at my over exaggeration, but it was impossible to forget the hatred in Eve's mother's gaze when she'd accused me. Queasiness rose through me each time I remembered the rest of the bystander's venomous stares at me.

I paced back and forth in my room, then collapsed on my bed. My heart beat frantically as I tried to think of anything else but Eve, which only ended up in my thoughts trailing to Daxon and Wilder. To their argument; and the fact that their hatred of each other seemed to be growing. Of course I was somehow being drawn to each because it seemed I liked to complicate my life.

Wilder had carried me back to my room yesterday, set me a bath, and then lay in bed next to me until I slept. No one had ever done that for me, and I wanted to make sure I never forgot. As much as he still remained a mystery and I had so much more to understand about him and this town, I appreciated him caring for me.

Now when it came to Daxon, I was torn and twisted.

He'd been so kind to me since arriving in town, but recently, he'd changed, growing darker, more mysterious.

My breath shuddered out of me at how confused I felt about these men.

For the tenth time this morning, I wondered how I could leave town without anyone seeing me.

Staring at the white ceiling, I found my thoughts drifted back to Eve, to her laughter, to her smile, then her dead body. My gut tightened.

This wasn't the first time I'd seen death. I wished I could say it was, but Alistair had made sure it was a frequent sight. He'd destroyed anyone he perceived to be a threat, which happened to be a lot of people. None of those experiences had softened the edge of seeing death or having it paraded in front of me though.

My eyes shut, and images floated in front of me, memories I hated, but stopping them was close to impossible.

"Sit the fuck still," Alistair barked in my face, all the while wrenching my arms behind me and around the chair's back, where he'd shoved me to sit. "You're shit at taking direction."

My eyes pricked with tears, but I refused to show him fear. That only got him more excited, made him more cruel. I had no clue what I did this time to set him off, and it didn't take much, I knew this, but my mind ran wild, trying to remember what it could be.

His face pushed into mine, and he smirked as he harshly tied my wrists up with the red ribbon I'd worn in my hair. "I told you before, Rune, about making yourself pretty for others. It comes with consequences. You don't fucking flirt with anyone," he spat. "You are mine, and I do what I like with you.

I make those decisions for you, not you. If I want someone to fuck you, then I'll make sure it happens under my watchful eye. You piss me off enough, and I'll get the whole fucking pack to fuck you." His hand struck toward me as fast as a viper. He grasped my throat and squeezed, and the pressure of his grip had me nodding in agreement. Right then, I'd agree to anything in order to be released. "So you, my little moon, seem to have forgotten your place today." He mocked me with his pet name, thinking it was hilarious. It made me ill each time he called me that. If he'd accepted me as his mate, I would have been his luna...his literal moon.

Now I was nothing but this.

I sucked in the shallow breaths he allowed, frozen in my seat, too terrified to make a single sound.

"Rune. Rune. Rune. What you did today was so damn stupid. You think I didn't see you wriggling your slutty ass as you walked past my room while I had a business meeting, then tying your hair up with that red ribbon." His lips curled with sinister menace, and my heart shivered at the notion that he was going to strike me in the face any second now. I tensed in my seat, waiting for it, bracing myself for the stinging ache. "You're in heat, I can smell it, and don't worry, after this, I'll make sure to take care of you."

Tears slid down my cheeks at his words, and a shiver started in the pit of my stomach as I knew exactly what that meant. Panic burned through me, and escape rolled over my mind, building like an unstoppable tornado. My heart beat so fast, it was ready to explode.

Except, he'd never let me get far.

Staring right into my eyes, he tsked. "Now I want you to know, what happens to Lester is all your fault, little moon. You made him look at you, and for that, I had no choice but to gouge out his eyes." He released my throat at once, and I gasped for air as terror clawed up my spine.

"Alistair, please, I just wanted to tie my hair up. It's hot today." Desperation trembled my words.

His fist came for me sudden and fast, clipping me just below the eye. The excruciating pain was immediate and jolted up my face like my skull was cracking in two. My bones seemed to shudder as my head flung backward from the impact, and I cried out from the unbearable sting. There was nothing but stars in my vision, nothing but a thundering pulse deep behind my eye.

"Don't ever talk back to me," he growled.

Holding back how badly I wanted to ugly cry from how much my face hurt, I turned my gaze from him, hating him with every fiber of my being. His meeting today went shit, as I'd heard the shouting from across the mansion. But I was also stupid to have even gone anywhere near them. I wasn't thinking and wanted to head into the backyard for fresh air, to stop listening to the yelling. I should have known better.

Furious at myself, at him, I kept my mouth shut, taking in raspy breaths while tears pooled in my eyes.

He wiped them from my cheeks with a thumb, and his attempt at tenderness only bristled my rage. My vision blurred in and out, but I tried to push past how half my face felt like it had swollen to the size of a puffer fish.

Then he pulled up, squaring his shoulders, and looked over to Lester, who was slumped in the corner of the basement. His soft whimpers were barely noticeable behind how loud my heart pounded in my ears. Lester lay on his side, his wrists and ankles tied behind him, while blood poured from his eye sockets. Silver coins were embedded in the sockets so that his shifter healing couldn't get to work. I cringed, lowering my gaze when Alistair grabbed my chin, squeezing so hard, I couldn't hold back the cry of pain that time.

I didn't care about him or any of Alistair's business acquaintances and friends. They could all die right at this moment, and I'd celebrate. He associated with no one but thugs and criminals. Amid them, my fated mate was the most evil person I'd ever met, and he delivered punishment to anyone who crossed him.

It was hard to imagine what I must have done for the moon goddess to think that the perfect true mate for me was him. I must have been a monster in another life.

"You will watch and know that next time you go against me, this will happen to you."

I nodded, shaking as I turned my attention to Lester, while my thoughts drowned in darkness, in my bleak life, and hatred.

"That's a good snowflake. You're learning. Maybe one day, you'll even beg me to kill someone for you."

The way he said those words, his voice almost brimming with excitement, only brought bile to the back of my throat. But I didn't respond, didn't dare, still he grinned, taking pleasure from terrifying me.

I swallowed the thickness in my throat, and instead of Lester, all I could picture was Alistair slumped on the ground, tied up, and how much easier my life would be if he was eliminated. Most nights, I dreamed of ways to get rid of him, the best way to destroy such a revolting beast. A blade in his heart while he slept. A gun to his head. But each time I woke, that determination dissolved into fear. Into the *reality that if he so much as suspected I was thinking I wanted him dead, he'd murder me in the most painful way possible.*

There was also that weak, desperate part of me that knew I'd never be able to kill someone who literally owned part of my soul.

Abruptly, Alistair broke into a chuckle, then clapped, and I flinched in my skin. "Let's do this already."

He marched across the basement to the table near the far wall and picked up the long thin samurai sword he'd brought downstairs with him. A chill spread through me, and a whimper rolled over my throat, which I regretted immediately.

He looked at me, his brows pulled together. "You better not cause me anymore trouble."

Swinging the sword through the air in a show of how well he handled the weapon, he grinned to himself, while I wanted to scream for him to release me. He walked over to Lester and stood over him. "Now, where were we before we got interrupted?"

The beta wolf shifter whimpered, blood smeared across his face and down the front of his chest from his gouged eyes. Maybe I was just as broken as everyone else in this house to feel such little pity for him. The longer I spent with Alistair, the more he completely destroyed me.

I tugged against the ribbon, my hands almost numb from how tightly he'd tied them up.

"We can make another deal," Lester slurred in response. "Come on, Alistair, I have a wife and two kids, I'd never look at your girl."

Alistair scoffed at his answer as he swung his blade up over his shoulder.

My heart pummeled against my ribcage, terror swallowing me. Everything about him disgusted and sickened me.

He glanced over his shoulder at me, making my skin crawl. "That's right, my moon. Keep watching."

In a heartbeat, the swift whisper of his sword came down on Lester fast, striking him across the soft flesh of his neck.

The blade bit into his skin, slicing all the way through so fast, I had no time to look away.

Lester gurgled, and his horrified cry ended abruptly.

Blood splashed across Alistair's shirt and the stone floor. Red dots stained everything around them.

I couldn't move or even breathe, too scared to say a damned thing. The way his head rolled backward, detached from the body, made me queasy. So much so, that in seconds, I threw up my breakfast all over the floor and across my shoes. Everything came out so fast, it left me dizzy.

"For fuck's sake, Rune."

The image of Lester's decapitated head was going to haunt me. I could already feel it sticking to my thoughts like a virus.

Alistair shook his head at me. "You're cleaning this whole fucking mess. Your putrid vomit, the blood, everything. Fuck me, you're such a weak bitch."

I shot up and out of bed, wrenched from the memory, my heart racing and my knees shaking.

I was never going to escape Alistair.

I would be haunted by him forever, until eventually, I went mad.

I trembled and rubbed the goosebumps out of my arms. Anytime I thought of him, I felt so dirty and guilty. I remember vomiting two more times during the cleanup in the basement, and I vowed to never go near Alistair's office ever again. But it didn't stop him torturing me at any chance he got.

There was so much vileness in everything he touched.

I took several steps toward the glaring sunlight pouring through the window and looked outside again to where nothing had changed from earlier. My mind buzzed, dragging me into panic about what I should do next. I needed to leave town, yet they wouldn't let me go. And now most of those living here would blame me for Eve's death. It made more sense from their perspective to blame the newcomer as opposed to an enemy no one had seen except me.

With my past haunting me, all that was left for me to desperately hold onto some normalcy in life and to some reason to keep fighting. Anger and fear tangled inside me, but another emotion had entered the battleground and seemed to be winning. Hopelessness.

I paced outside the inn, listening to the sounds coming from within and resisting the urge to tear the front door off the handles and throw it at the next guy's voice I heard.

Rune was in there.

And I was out here, going out of my mind. My skin felt itchy, like something was crawling underneath it. Almost how it had felt right before my first shift.

My wolf had long since settled, most of the time feeling one with me instead of a separate entity. But right now...my wolf was on its own, bucking at my insides as he tried to convince me I needed to go inside.

What if she was with another man? The thought felt like a knife burning through my insides. I could just picture her, sitting by the bar, sipping her drink with that sweet little smile of hers. The one that had every wolf in this village wanting to come out here.

Was she wearing a flirty, little dress where every male in the place could have a nice, long look at those fucking sexy legs of hers? Were they imagining those legs wrapped around them?

The thought was too much for me. If it had been a full moon, I would have shifted right now. She was mine. *Ours*, my wolf stubbornly insisted.

Fuck. No. She wasn't mine.

That lie was enough to make me lose control. A snarl ripped through my chest, and I punched the heavy wooden door, barely feeling the shards cutting at my skin. The door flew open, pieces of wood flying everywhere. I stormed inside, ready to rip Rune from the arms of the stupid man with a death wish that she was with.

There was no sign of Rune, however. There were just a bunch of flabbergasted members of my pack looking at me like I'd lost my mind.

Which I had. Obviously.

Jim was behind the bar, frozen in place, a scowl all over his face since I'd just somehow managed to punch a hole through his extremely thick front door. Which honestly in retrospect, was shocking even to me. I knew I was strong...but not that strong.

Rune. The urge to see her nearly knocked me over. I looked around the room, desperate to see her. It wasn't a want, it was a need at this point. A compulsion.

A thought crossed my mind. A ridiculous thought. One that filled me with dread. If I was in control of myself at all at this moment, I would be running away as far as I could. I would never set eyes on Rune again.

But I wasn't in control anymore, was I?

When I saw she wasn't anywhere, my gaze flickered to the staircase, wondering how crazy it would be if I went up to her room. Just to check on her of course. That's all it would be.

Because what I thought was happening, it wasn't happening. I wouldn't let it happen.

I stumbled towards the stairs, feeling like I was drunk...wishing I was drunk and that could explain how out of control I was.

I made it to the landing and gripped the handrail like it could prevent me from going further forward. I reluctantly let go when the bearings that connected the railing to the wall started to groan as they threatened to give way. I was already going to have to make sure Jim and Carrie got a new front door. I probably shouldn't make it a stair rail as well.

It felt like my wolf was dragging me towards Rune's door. Terror, desire...fear, they were all coursing through my veins.

I pounded on the door, furious with myself, but unable to drag my body away.

Just a look, I told myself. I just needed to look at her. Then I could leave.

My wolf rumbled under my skin, almost like he was laughing at me. The asshole.

"Open the door, Rune. It's me, Wilder," I practically growled. I cringed at what a psycho I sounded like. But this was her fault! She was the one doing this to me.

There was a long pause, and I literally had to clench my fists to prevent myself from pounding on the door again and demanding that she let me in.

Finally, she opened it. I exhaled a breath of relief as I

soaked her in. Fuck, she was the most stunning thing I'd ever fucking seen in my life.

Mine, my wolf reminded me.

"Wilder?" she asked with a raised eyebrow. I realized she must have asked me something, and I'd been too busy devouring every perfect feature on her body to hear it.

"Um, hey," I responded lamely.

We both stood there awkwardly, until finally, she swung the door farther open. My insides erupted into flames as she motioned for me to step inside.

"Wilder, what are you doing here?" she said softly. Rune looked exhausted. Peering at her closer, I could tell she had dark circles under her eyes, like she hadn't been sleeping.

"What's wrong?" I asked, intentionally not answering her question.

She fidgeted in place and let out a soft breath. "Nothing," she lied.

Awkward silence once again descended.

My gaze continued to eat her up. Fuck, I wanted her so bad. I could picture every inch of her body naked right now. I began to grow painfully hard just thinking about what it had been like to touch her last time. Her eyes widened as she delicately sniffed the air. Hmm, she could smell my lust. We'd have to examine that closer later. Because right now...

Rune caught me completely off guard when she suddenly leaped forward and lifted her face to mine and kissed me. What little was left of my self-control snapped with the simple caress of her mouth. A growl ripped free from my throat, and I parted her lips with my tongue, licking into the sweetness. Fuck, I couldn't get enough. She tasted like strawberries, and fuck me, the scent of vanilla and caramel wrapped around me until all I could breathe was her.

She moaned softly as she melted against me. Her hands stroked up my chest, the feel of her sending sparks across my skin. My heart stuttered as I gripped her ass in my hands and lifted her so I could kiss her deeper, slanting my mouth over hers again and again as I carried her to the bed on the other side of the room. I sat her gently down on it and leaned forward over her as her legs wrapped around my waist.

Heat seared me through my clothes. It was like our combined lust had transformed into flames that were determined to burn me from the inside out. My cock screamed for relief.

"Wilder," she groaned against my lips. I tangled a hand into her silky hair and kissed her harder, pressing myself against her like I could somehow convince her to be permanently attached to me.

That wasn't a weird thing to think at all.

Kissing her felt dangerous. Everything about her felt dangerous right now though. This pull I was feeling, it had the power to destroy me. To destroy everything I'd worked so hard to build my whole life. I could already feel her taking over, her essence spreading through me until I knew she was all I'd care about eventually.

It was already happening.

She gripped my hair, using it to hold me to her as I kissed her over and over, driving every breathless sigh I could from her lungs with swirls and slides of my tongue.

Don't go any further. Keep your clothes on. I repeated the mantra, keeping my mouth on hers, but it didn't stop my body from getting desperate for the need to feel more of her. Her hips rocked into mine, and I shivered, unable to stop myself from sliding my hand under her dress and up her thigh. I couldn't do anything but groan as my wolf waged a war inside of me to do more...to claim her.

My mate.

Her skin was the stuff of wet dreams, so soft and smooth, I was half convinced that she couldn't be real. I had the insane urge to mar her skin, to mark it with my bites so that everyone could see she belonged to me.

"Rune," I groaned, tugging her closer, grinding myself against the soft heat between her thighs, the ache of wanting her almost too much.

Every touch was like a drug, triggering some undeniable, primal possessiveness that threatened to rage out of control.

I needed to stop, take a step back, breathe some fresh air that didn't fucking consist of her scent alone. I was going to do something crazy, like actually bite her. My eyes rolled to the back of my head just thinking about it.

Claim her, my wolf ordered, snarling at me to just do it. I pulled back from the kiss, my breath coming out in gasps. How was it possible I felt this turned on, and we hadn't done anything yet aside from kiss?

Mate, the voice inside of me screamed again. The word burned inside of me. I'd known I wanted her. I'd known that I was growing more and more obsessed with her every day. But there was a difference between choosing to be with someone you were crazy about, and suddenly having to be with someone you were crazy about because you didn't have any other choice.

"Why are you stopping?" she whispered, chasing my lips with her own.

"I shouldn't be here," I groaned, even as I sipped from her lips like they were some exotic wine. I rolled my hips against hers again, wishing the layers of fabric between us would simply disappear.

"Probably not," she agreed, but she made no move to push me away. If anything, she pulled me closer, like she was just as desperate for me as I was for her. Which honestly didn't seem possible because I couldn't imagine any other person being capable of wanting something as much as this.

She pulled back a bit, those piercing blue eyes locked with mine, her lips parted and swollen from my kisses.

"More," she murmured. My grip tightened on her thigh, my thumb traveling to graze the edge of what felt like lace.

"It's different this time," I said, trying to warn her, knowing she would have to be the one to stop us. My mouth was literally throbbing at the thought of giving her a mating mark. And we needed to talk about it first, but I was having trouble thinking of anything but the fact that she smelled so fucking good, she kissed so fucking good, she felt so fucking good.

"I just want to feel you. I need to feel you," Rune moaned, and my heartbeat got faster because she sounded desperate too. Maybe she was feeling what I was.

Except I didn't want that. Had never wanted that.

Her lips passed over mine again, and once again, my thoughts drifted away. Rune cradled the back of my head as if I was something precious and drew me closer. My lips brushed her skin, and I kissed her gently as need roared within me.

"Make me feel," she ordered. "Make me forget." Her second statement was so soft, it was almost unspoken, but of course with my wolf senses, I heard every word. My insides dropped at her words. Was she here with me? Or was she thinking of someone else right now, just using me to get off since she couldn't have him?

When exactly had I turned into such a pussy?

Determination scored through my veins. I didn't care if she was thinking of someone else. By the end of this, she would only be thinking of me, dreaming of me, craving me...just as much as I craved her.

Her heartbeat quickened, as if she could sense what I was thinking, but her grip only tightened. Her hips undulated against mine frantically. My cock strained against my pants. I really needed to rethink skinny jeans after this. Maybe get off the wannabe rocker look I'd been trying the last fifty years. My balls would probably thank me.

I wanted to consume her in every way, to bury myself deep inside her. My hand slid between her thighs, and she parted them wider, urging me closer. My thumb pressed into her cleft through her underwear, and I growled without breaking my hold, the sound low and deep in my chest. She wasn't just wet, she was soaked through the fabric of her panties. I pushed the lace against her clit, and she gasped. Her kiss turned even sweeter and more addictive as her desperation grew. I moved my thumb in a steady rhythm that echoed her soft moans and the brush of our lips. I hoisted her up in my arms, and her thighs tightened around my hips.

"Wilder...please." She ran her hand under my shirt, her fingers stroking up over my abs to my chest. She chanted my name, and I scraped my nail across the fabric covering her, eliciting another fucking gorgeous gasp.

I pinched, and she groaned, her thighs trembling. I pressed and rubbed, and she came apart, screaming my name and going limp against me.

Her body still shuddered as I set her down and then sank to my knees in front of her, tracing the band of her underwear with my tongue. The scent of her drove me slowly mad...but what a way to go.

I looked up at her, and she was watching me, that wild look in her gaze like she was either about to run or fucking explode. She gripped the bottom of her dress and slowly, maddeningly, slipped it over her head. The fucking sexiest strip tease I'd ever seen, and she hadn't even shown me the good stuff yet.

Her breathing was harsh as she reached behind her back. I could hear every single hook slip free as she removed her bra and dropped it to the ground beside us.

"I feel like I'm dying when I look at you," I growled, my voice almost unrecognizable it was so heavy with lust. "You're so fucking perfect. An angel sent to drag me down to hell."

Her breasts swayed above me, just begging to be played with, as Rune slid the red thong she was wearing down her legs achingly slow.

Finally, they fell to the ground and she was naked.

Mine, my wolf growled, and this time, I wanted to argue with him because the goddess standing in front of me was most assuredly mine.

She stared down at me, almost challenging, like she could sense my turmoil and desire and she was trying to see how far she could push me towards the edge.

The need to claim her in every way possible spiked through my body, pushing away absolutely every fucking rational thought I'd had about what was happening.

I grabbed her hips and buried my face between her thighs, stabbing my tongue through her folds to taste her. I moaned, long and loud, as she gasped, her nails digging into my shoulders as she gripped me tightly. I pushed her thighs apart for a better angle, then moved my tongue deeper, dragging my tongue over her clit with each slide.

"Wilder!" she practically screamed. That dark voice inside of me wanted to see how loud I could make her, just to make sure anyone who was around knew she was taken.

She began to rock against me, riding my tongue as I spread her with my fingers and stroked and rubbed at her clit. I thrust inside her with first one finger, and then two, stretching her tight muscles with each stroke. Her knees shook, but I still continued to feast on her cries and the fucking perfect taste of her pussy as I added a third finger. She was so wet, I knew I could take her right now and claim her, but some sadistic part of me wanted to see how desperate I could make her.

"Wilder, please." She collapsed against me as her breath quickened, and the movement of her hips grew frantic.

"You're almost there, aren't you, sweetheart?" I murmured against her skin, right as I sucked hard on her clit.

She screamed and came around my fingers in waves. My hand and my mouth were flooded with her sweet taste. I couldn't help but lick her clean as she came through her orgasm. A moment passed, and she went limp against me. She looked down at me, a smirk on her perfect fucking face as she stared dreamily at me.

"Your mouth is incredible," she purred. "Every part of you is incredible."

I kissed her roughly, letting her taste herself, then stood back and quickly stripped out of my clothes. She lay there on the bed, a vision against the pale sheets with her hair strewn everywhere, a flush in her cheeks and her lips swollen and pouty.

"Eat a donut," she murmured as her gaze ate me up as I stalked across the bed to hover over her. "You're making the rest of us look bad."

Her fingers began to explore the lines of my chest and stomach. She followed her fingers with her tongue, and I bit down on my lip, trying to quell the urge to take over and rut into her. Her hands eventually reached my cock, and I cursed as her fingers wrapped around my dick. Just that single touch was enough to send pleasure ripping down my spine, the intensity of it a warning of just how close I was to losing my control.

My wolf let out a frustrated growl inside of me, and I closed my eyes and tried to count to ten to get ahold of myself.

"Rune, I think I'm going to have to let you play later," I warned.

"Now that doesn't sound fun," she said wickedly. My eyes widened at the sass my shy girl was giving me. Half the time, I felt like she was trying to hide away in the shadows, and I had to drag her to my side. I pinned her wrists above her head with one hand and gave her a low growl that cut off her cute giggle.

Did I just say cute? Fuck. She was ruining me.

Mate, my wolf reminded me again.

"Behave," I warned her. "I'm too close." I knew she interpreted my statement as meaning I was going to blow at any second...which could have been the truth too. But I really meant that it was taking everything inside of me not to bite into her pretty skin and claim her as my mate once and for all.

My eyes dropped to the sensual lines of her throat and shoulder. I shook my head, trying to clear the haze of lust settling over me. Rune parted her thighs, and I sank between them, savoring the thread of anticipation slicing down my spine at what was about to come.

I gave her one more deep kiss on her lips before I began to kiss my way down her neck, licking and nibbling at her skin until she was once more panting and writhing beneath me.

"Please, please, please," she pleaded, shaking her

head as she tried to use her legs to get me where she wanted me.

I released her hands, and her fingers immediately stroked over my shoulders, my arms, anywhere she could reach. "Are you mine, my pretty girl?" I asked as I lazily ran my tongue over her nipple, then sucked it into my mouth.

She groaned, rocking her hips. "I hate you," she breathed. I just chuckled darkly as I shook my head, then moved to her other breast, sucking at her nipple with my mouth and tongue before lifting my head.

Her eyes were glittering with desperate need.

"You should try begging some more," I teased as I worked her breasts until she was arching towards me and her peaks were swollen and red.

She let out a sharp growl underneath me, and I froze for a second. It sounded very...wolflike. Rune didn't seem to know what she'd done as she was still begging and pleading under me. I put her growl as yet another thing we'd need to be discussing after this.

I licked and sucked at every inch of her stomach, memorizing the curves I'd hopefully get to spend the rest of my life worshipping. Her hips rolled rhythmically under me, and I was finding it harder and harder to hold out. I didn't know who this was teasing more— me or her. I thrust my hips once, sliding through her slick folds and stroking her clit with the head of my cock.

"Wilder," she cried, digging into my back and leaving marks that I wished my supernatural healing would leave.

"Shhh. Not yet, sweetheart. You don't want it enough yet."

She screamed something unintelligible under me that I swallowed with another kiss to her lips.

I stroked her clit with my thumb, and she cried out again. Her hips lifted, and her begging only increased as she tried to drop over the edge. I pet her in small circles before finally taking pity on her and giving her the exact pressure she needed to come apart again. Her head thrashed as she came, her body stiffening under me.

"You're so fucking beautiful, Rune," I growled out.

She gazed at me with wild, frantic eyes, and I had to be in her. Rune consumed me. She was all I could see...all I could feel. I lined up my cock at her entrance and took a deep breath before driving forward in one powerful thrust and seating myself to the hilt.

She cried out and immediately came again. I gritted my teeth and stiffened, trying to stop myself from falling after her.

Mate, my wolf and I once again agreed.

That unease flickered inside of me again, the one that had hated the thought of a mate and felt it akin to a jail sentence. But I pushed it aside and tried to focus on what she felt like at that moment. Like the best fucking thing I'd ever experienced. She was so fucking tight...and so wet. My dick was in heaven...as was the rest of me. Balancing myself on my forearms, I locked every muscle in my body to keep control, fighting the urge to go fast as I slowly reared back and slid in again.

"You good, baby?" I purred as sweat beaded on my skin from the effort.

"So good," she moaned, thrashing her head once again as we both fell under a wave of sensations. She cupped the back of my neck with one hand, skimming her fingers down the side of my face with the other. I thrust again, my stomach tightening with each curl of my body as I clung to the tiny scraps of reason that reminded me I couldn't lose myself. I couldn't just bite her.

I set the pace with deep, hard, slow strokes that sent exquisite pleasure spiraling through my body. Our breaths grew unsteady as sweat slicked our skin. I didn't know how this was better than the last time, but it somehow was. Every thrust was better. Every time I filled her, it felt insanely hotter.

I would never get enough of this...of her. Fuck, imagine how good it would be once we had a lot of practice. I grinned at the thought before I pressed another fierce kiss against her lips. I felt her began to grow tight beneath me.

"That's it, baby," I murmured. Her eyes fluttered shut, and I memorized her every feature while I had the chance to look uninterrupted.

"You're mine," I couldn't help but growl again, my voice like shattered glass.

She opened her eyes, and I saw something defiant in her gaze, like she'd decided no matter what, I'd never own every part of her.

That wouldn't do.

My self-control snapped, and I drove into her again and again until she came yet again, her body convulsing around mine. She pulled me over that edge with her, pleasure charging down my spine until I exploded, my vision going black only to erupt in a kaleidoscope of colors. I bit into her shoulder mindlessly before getting ahold of myself and quickly releasing her.

She stiffened beneath me as I horrifyingly watched a few pinpricks of blood fall down her shoulder.

"What did you just do?" she asked hoarsely, her voice gone from all the screaming I'd made her do over the last hour or so we'd been in here.

"Just got a little excited," I quickly said, even as nerves settled into my gut. I hadn't initiated the mating bond, I knew that. But what I'd done... Fuck.

"Okayyyy," she said tiredly. Rune slowly relaxed beneath me, her breath steadying, even as I tried to resist my wolf's order to bite her again.

Rune was reducing me to truly nothing but an animal, a reason that I'd always dreaded the mating bond to begin with.

I rolled to the side, taking her with me as I pulled her against my chest. The room was silent but for our soft breaths and the pounding of both of our hearts. I swallowed, anticipation and dread coursing through me as I prepared to broach the subject of what I thought was happening. Of what I knew was happening.

She'd want to be mine. I knew she would. What we'd just experienced...it was nothing short of magical. Fated. Written in the stars and all that other bullshit people always said when they were talking about their mates.

Rune lazily traced nonsensical shapes on my chest. "Why are you so tense?" she whispered softly. "I thought orgasms were supposed to relax you."

"I just need to talk to you about something," I said

against her hair as I inhaled its scent like a lovestruck fool.

She stiffened against me. "Please don't tell me you're about to give me a 'it's not you, it's me' kind of talk. Because that would really suck."

I snorted, thinking how off the mark she was.

"I'm beginning to feel the mating bond," I finally reluctantly told her.

She was completely still for what felt like an hour until she scrambled away from me like I was a snake about to strike.

"You're starting the mating bond with another girl and you're here with me?" she growled hoarsely, disgust written all over her pretty features.

"What? No!" I told her indignantly as I reached for her. This was not how I envisioned this going.

"Then what are you talking about? What mating bond?"

"A mating bond with you!" I snapped.

If anything, the disgust on her face only deepened. Her disgust...and her fear.

"That's not possible," she said as she jumped from the bed frantically and began to throw her clothes on.

"Rune—" I murmured, getting off the bed and walking toward her beseechingly.

She held up her hands to stop me, her eyes wild and out of control. "I have a mate," she told me, the reminder a brutal blow.

"You told me you didn't belong to him. You know we belong together. Tell me you feel it," I said beseechingly, grabbing at my hair as I stood there butt naked.

"I had a mate, and he rejected me. I don't get another chance," she said coldly.

And admittedly, I hadn't heard of this happening... but the more time that passed, the more I knew. The mating bond was happening.

"Rune, baby. Just relax. We'll figure this all out, but it's happening. And I'm going to make sure you never regret it."

She looked utterly destroyed standing there, a beautiful, heartbreaking figure with her sex blown hair and her red, swollen lips. "I can't belong to you when I still belong to him," she said sadly.

It felt like she'd stabbed me right in the heart as I soaked in the reality of what she was saying.

"Then I guess I'll have to make sure I change that," I finally answered before grabbing my clothes and stalking out of the room.

I slammed the door behind me and slipped on my clothes before anyone saw, although obviously, nudity was nothing in a place like this filled with shifters.

I made a vow as I went down the stairs and slipped outside. Rune was going to be mine. No matter what. Even if I had to kill her bastard of a mate to ensure that.

I inhaled sharply as anxiety burned through me.

I remained frozen in my bedroom, staring out the window at nothing, yet at the same time, my mind buzzed about everything that had happened lately.

A mating bond with you.

Wilder's words spiraled in my mind.

I'd already found my mate, he knew this already. He'd been a monster, but he was my soulmate. The moon goddess only gave you one. My wolf had already made her choice to the point that even now when I thought of Alistair, a painfully dark loneliness tore through me. It was a strange thing to miss someone to the point that it felt like I might die from the agony, yet detest him with every fiber of my being.

The way Wilder had looked at me as he left had me shivering. He was determined to prove me wrong, to push ahead with this crazy idea he'd come up with. What did it say about me that I only ever ended up with crazy people? The reality of that was like a sledgehammer to my chest.

I closed my eyes and held onto the window frame. Tears squeezed out of the corners of my eyes. Alistair had left me so broken that when a gorgeous man wanted to claim me, I panicked instead of embracing it.

For a second, I allowed myself to dream of a world where I'd met Wilder first, where he had been my true mate.

But even that was terrifying to think about with how damaged Alistair had left me.

If I was being honest with myself, I didn't know that I could ever be connected so closely to anyone again. I didn't know that I could ever allow myself to lose my control. I didn't know that I could ever let myself go enough to give Wilder...or Daxon the connection they seemed to be looking for.

Of course I realized the hypocrisy of my vagina desperately wanting Wilder's body, yet the mention of being bonded left me shaken.

Every time I thought of Wilder, I melted. When he kissed me, I was ready to destroy the world to remain in his arms. But for our souls to be entwined, the very essence of who we were to merge, was a very different matter. One that I wasn't sure was possible, or if I wanted to go through with again.

I wiped my cheeks, more confused than ever. Maybe what I needed was fresh air, to get out of the room that felt like it suffocated me.

As I grabbed fresh clothes from my dresser, my mind still replayed images of Wilder coming into my room and ravaging me. Why couldn't he be like every other asshole out there and just be interested in great sex? That sounded much safer to me.

I buttoned up my jeans and pulled on a faded blue blouse with long sleeves. The neckline was so loose, it hung over a shoulder. Luckily, I had recently bought a strapless bra from the local store in town and could pull it off. Taking another quick look at myself in the mirror, I decided I looked relatively normal and as non-threatening as I could make myself in preparation for crossing paths with locals.

I pushed my white-blonde hair into a ponytail, with a few loose strands framing my face, then I stepped outside my room and headed downstairs. Night had crawled into the hallway, and it seemed especially quiet.

Downstairs, the inn was empty. Not a soul in sight... well, except for Jim, who owned Lair Inn.

"Evening, Rune," he greeted me from behind the bar he was wiping down. "Are you hungry? There's some of Carrie's Irish lamb stew left." His smile warmed me and had always made me feel safe from the first day I stumbled into his establishment.

My stomach growled on cue, and I laughed at how loud it sounded. "Apparently, I'm very hungry." Then I glanced to both ends of the bar. Chairs and tables were everywhere, the windows and door shut, but not a soul in sight. "I'm surprised it's so quiet here," I said, remembering how packed the inn got only a few nights ago, which also ended in a huge brawl between Daxon and Wilder.

"Most are at the town hall tonight. Carrie's down there too."

I met Jim's green eyes, the light overhead brightening his short, silver hair, giving him a soft expression, but there was no denying the shadow behind his gaze.

"Is there a convention in town?" I teased, but as the words left my mouth, I couldn't help but wonder if it had everything to do with Eve's death. Were they talking about me and how to kick me out of town? Were they going to send a mob after me?

I obviously had a really active imagination.

My heart lunged into my ribs, the earlier grief and worry colliding through me, and my fingers trembled as they caught the bottom of my shirt nervously.

Jim's brow narrowed. "Sit and I'll bring you some food. It will do you good."

The thought of food made me sick suddenly. To know that so many people were together, likely talking about me, felt like a blade twisting in my gut. And why didn't Wilder tell me about it earlier? I could only assume the meeting was a last-minute decision.

"Thank you, but I don't think I could eat a thing right now." Maybe it was all in my head, a figment of my imagination, but as I lifted my gaze to Jim once more, the worry on his face confirmed my worst fears. "I need to go," I said and turned away from him hastily, hurrying for the door. No matter what everyone thought, I had a right to defend myself.

"Rune," Jim called out behind me, and I looked over my shoulder at him. "I don't believe you were responsible for Eve's death. But sometimes, fear and panic make people desperate and jump to conclusions. Be careful out there, as not everyone is thinking straight right now."

I swallowed the lump in my throat and gave him a quick nod, unable to find my words. I slipped outside into the cool night that pressed in around me. For several long moments, I stood beneath the main inn lights, trying to catch my breath and calm my racing heart.

I'd only been in town for a few weeks, but I'd like to think I hadn't come across as a major psycho. Despite that the locals were quick to believe I was capable of such a brutal attack. I shook my head in frustration.

Several long breaths, and I turned toward the main road, where the lights were bright and chased away shadows.

The town hall was located at the end of the main street, and as much as trepidation wormed its way through my gut, I never stopped heading in that direction. I practically ran there, my pulse on fire as anger brewed in my chest. Eve had meant something to me, I'd had no reason to kill her.

I passed row after row of closed stores, and even the coffee shop and diner were shut, which meant a lot as that place never seemed to close. My strides lengthened the more my mind imagined what I was about to find. A voice in my head was screaming at me that I was giving them the chance they were looking for to come after me.

I pushed the voice away.

I wanted the shifters living in this town to understand I wasn't guilty. I could barely bring myself to harm a bug, and seeing as I couldn't even change into my wolf, I had yet to experience my primal killing instincts that usually came with a wolf's first shift.

Still, Jim's warning swam in my head about people being irrational when they were upset.

Up ahead, the town hall rose into view, a dark brick building with a pointy roof the color of midnight covered in a generous topping of green lichen. Long arched windows gave the place an appearance of a long forgotten church, and maybe it had once been a place of worship before the wolves moved into the town of Amarok.

Bright light blazed from the windows, and I could see the shadows of all the people moving around inside. In the front yard, I froze, dragging my eyes over the front door that remained shut. Doubt crawled over me, telling me I should turn back. Before I could change my mind, I marched up the three stone steps to the grand double doors and placed my hand on the iron handle. I pressed my ear to the door. Voices escalated inside, but no particular one stood out for me to work out who exactly spoke.

Licking my lips, I pushed down the handle slowly and eased the door ajar before I peered inside. The room was packed. Rows and rows of chairs lined the large assembly room, all facing the front stage, where a tall, blond man I didn't recognize stood, talking to the crowd quite angrily by the look of his shaking fist in the air. Nearly every chair was taken right to the back of the room, and I figured even if I tried to stealthy sneak inside now, I'd be spotted instantly.

I scanned the faces, recognizing Carrie from the inn right away, sitting by the far corner, but from my angle, it was hard to see her expression. Miyu and her boyfriend,

Rae, sat toward the back. She had her arms folded across her chest, looking perturbed. Most townsfolk I recognized were scattered among the others I haven't yet had the chance to meet.

"We vote on her guilt then," the man on the stage announced, grabbing my attention.

My stomach twisted, and my whole body shook. I had a feeling I knew who they were talking about.

"That's not going to happen," a deeply gravelly voice spoke out, and everyone in the room fell silent.

Wilder stepped into view as he approached the speaker. He stood tall, and fury thinned his lips. He wore faded jeans and a tucked in, buttoned-up dark shirt. Seeing him had my heart fluttering, every part of me craving him...even in the midst of all of this. I'd never been touched and adored and fucked the way he had done to me, and the memory of what he did to me in my bedroom would remain with me forever.

"I've let you all have your say, but now this is ridiculous. We have no evidence Rune killed Eve, yet most of you are ready to hang her for the crime. She said she'd witnessed someone else at the crime scene, so that is the lead we will follow. We will set up hunting teams and go out searching the surrounding woods, along with questioning any local suspects."

The murmur of voices escalated quickly, most talking among themselves.

"This is insane, Wilder. Are you now trying to say one of us killed our very own Eve?" a woman called out from the crowd, her voice shaking with anger.

Eve's mother howled with cries from the front row,

while the woman next to her embraced her. That was when I realized I hadn't yet seen Daniel in the crowd.

Everyone broke into louder chatter, their accusations used as swords aimed at maiming me, some of them getting up, looking ready to challenge Wilder. Instead, they threw more questions and accusations at him. My heart beat faster, and I felt myself fall a little more at the way he was standing up for me. I certainly hadn't had a lot of that in my life.

An ear-piercing whistle cut through the noise. "Enough and sit your asses down," Daxon barked, his voice dark and authoritative, coming from somewhere to my right where I couldn't see the back of the hall.

All those standing instantly flopped back down as if his command was law, and a heavy blanket of silence fell over the room.

Daxon emerged into my line of sight, approaching Wilder at the front of the crowd. He was dressed in dark jeans and a long-sleeved tee, his muscles filling out his clothes. He was freaking beautiful in that dangerous kind of way that told me I shouldn't feel anything for him. "We can't lose our heads, even if we don't agree with Wilder's draconian approach." He then turned to Wilder and whispered something just between them.

Whatever he said caused Wilder's nostrils to flare and his shoulders bunched up, his eyes alight with fury.

My heartbeat sped up, having seen that look last time the two exchanged blows in the inn.

"I'm getting really sick of your shit," Wilder spat back at Daxon, and now the two were facing each other, seemingly forgetting the rest of the town watched. Maybe they didn't care, as this was how it had been between the two powerhouses for what seemed like a very long time.

A scraping sound came from behind me, and my veins turned to ice as I whipped around.

Darkness greeted me, and the wind blew a piece of garbage down the road. I closed my eyes for a second. *Calm down, Rune.*

It was hard enough breathing as I spied on the town residents wanting to condemn me, let alone every little sound now making me jump. The tips of my fingers curled as I jammed them into the pockets of my jeans and turned back to the door.

An explosion of growls echoed from inside so suddenly, I flinched backward. My heartbeat boomed.

Thundering sounds and growls came from within the room, the screech of chairs against the floorboards resonated, and someone even screamed.

I rushed forward, not thinking, and pushed open the door to the town hall. I stood in the doorway, my mouth agape as I stared at the chaotic war that had taken over a room where seconds earlier, there had been only calm.

People were on their feet, some pushing away from the front stage while others ran toward it. My legs trembled, but for once, I ignored my fear and ran forward. Already, I caught glimpses of Daxon and Wilder in a fight, punches flying, blood spilled. My stomach plummeted, my heart crushing beneath the weight of dread. I didn't want them fighting for me... They had to stop before someone got hurt.

Goosebumps raced up my arms as I shoved past people who ran in every direction.

Someone snatched my arm and squeezed, glaring down at me with disgust. "Are you happy now?" He spat the words at me, his fingers digging into my flesh.

I winced and pulled against him. "Let me go."

"You'll bring our town to its knees and destroy it."

"I didn't kill Eve," I retorted, sick and tired of being wrongly accused.

"Maybe you didn't, but it didn't stop you from igniting a flame between the two Alphas of this town. And now they'll burn down the place and all of us in it to claim you as their own. As far as I'm concerned, you might as well have killed that poor girl, as you'll send us all to our deaths."

Well, that seemed a bit dramatic.

I shuddered anyway, my legs weakening beneath me as the crowd stole the man from my sight.

I tried to swallow, to think straight, but it was difficult with all the insanity around me.

Boots tapped the floorboards around me as people ran and tried to leave the town hall, while others only gathered around the battle instead of stopping it.

My skin pricked with electricity, with the magic of a wolf's transformation. I jerked my head up to the sight of Wilder and Daxon in their wolf forms. They were enormous and terrifying, Daxon's fur white as snow, while Wilder was the color of midnight. They were the opposite in every possible way. Lips peeled back, ears pressed flat against their heads, they lunged at each other, crashing like two mountains going to war.

Desperation shoved me forward, and I speared

through the throng of people in my way. I had to reach
Wilder and Daxon to put a stop to this.

I wasn't the kind of girl these two should be fighting
over. They'd clearly lost their minds.

I finally stumbled free from the crowd and burst into
the circle watching the fight. Most cheered, others
growled like they waited for the signal to join in. Was
everyone mad in this town?

"Stop," I bellowed, my throat raw and my eyes
stinging.

Wilder's gaze snapped in my direction, a threatening
growl in his throat, one for me to back away. I knew that
sound all too well. Blood seeped from the side of his
head, but he wasn't relenting.

Daxon took that moment to smash into Wilder, and in
a split second, they hit the ground, entwined with one
another, fur and fangs and blood all I could see. Rivulets
of red were left in their wake, staining the floorboards.

The air was charged with rage, and I let out a sudden
cry, anything to grab their attention, to reach their damn
ears. "Please, stop fighting." My words came out choked,
just as Wilder took a sharp bite of Daxon's neck.

Their fierce battle had me lunging toward them. I
knew better than to try to stop fighting wolves. But my
head spun with confusion, with anger, with grief, and I
ran right into Wilder's side, my hands shoving into his
ribs with enough force to dislodge him from Daxon.

I recoiled just as fast, but not quick enough as Wilder
spun around, savagery in his eyes. In that same moment, he
lunged at me, something changed his eyes, something so

deep, that I recognized the human side of him seeing me for who I was at the last moment...not an enemy. In that minuscule split second when my heart attempted to burst out of my chest and panic froze me in the spot at him coming at me, we both knew there was no way he could pull back.

He slammed into my gut with the force of a tank, and I flew backward, crashing into the spectators, catching my fall. I cried out from the agony that emptied my lungs of oxygen.

Wilder stumbled and hit the ground, tripping over with me. I gasped for air, tangled with him and those bystanders we'd crashed into. Something sharp scraped and tore into my arm so fast and painfully, I cried out and flinched back.

But everything happened too fast after that. One moment, I lost my footing, and the next, Wilder flew back toward Daxon, who came at him with the full force of a tornado.

I scrambled back to my feet while those around me growled their anger, and someone even shoved me in the back. But I didn't care about them. Frustration and anger poured through me at how powerless I was to do anything about...well, anything.

I glanced down to my arm to where the red rolled down my hand and over my fingers, blood dripping to the floor. A great gash had torn my skin from Wilder's accidental attack. But with it, something inside me shifted, something I'd never felt before.

A sudden boom of snarls rocked the room, and I wrenched my head up to see Daxon throwing Wilder down to the ground. The crowd cheered, thrusting their fists into the air.

A fiery anger rose through me, overwhelming and destructive. I glanced around, lower members of the two packs who were not near the fight looked scared for their lives.

The click of nails hitting the floorboards rang as the pair kept fighting. These two were relentless.

I was pushed and shoved as people continued to clamor around me. "Fuck off," someone threw at me.

I stumbled backward and into someone else who nudged me aside.

Fire erupted within me, unfamiliar and overwhelming. I felt ready to rip someone apart.

Darkness took me over, stealing all the light inside me. In its place, a silence permeated in my head. The kind that shook me, that had me sensing my wolf like never before.

A brush of fur. A growl. A fury unlike anything I've ever felt. The wound on my arm stabbed deep, making me wince. When the two alphas rolled right past me, I screamed my fury.

"Stop!" The room seemed to tremble beneath me with how hard I breathed and trembled, with a scorching heat licking the back of my neck.

My insides clenched tight as so many feelings punched me in the gut, leaving me ragged. When someone knocked me aside, I snapped my head up, my teeth gnashing, lips pulled back at them.

The edges of my visions feathered, and I had no idea what was happening to me. The room spun, and I gripped the back of a chair for balance. I'd worked myself up so much, it felt like I'd lost control.

Something new lingered in the air. I tasted it on the back of my throat, bitter and metallic.

I burned up, my breaths sawing in and out of my chest, my injured arm stinging horrendously. While in my chest, fury bubbled to the point where I wanted to rip my own skin off to unleash my wolf, to tear into someone, to feel the warm trickle of blood on my throat.

Something was happening to me.

A sudden, excruciating jab to the side had me crying out, and I turned to see someone had tossed a chair at me. Around me, everyone else in the town hall had now turned on each other, throwing chairs and punches alike. The battle grew fierce, and the air was tainted with so much hatred, I had to get out before I was the one who did something crazy. On cue, my lips curled as if something else controlled me.

Even Carrie was fighting, except the scene around me was very wrong. She didn't seem the kind to take on someone half her age, but her growls and wolf eyes promised death.

"Carrie," I called to her. "Don't do this. You need to get out of here. Everyone needs to fucking stop this."

But the louder my voice grew, the more they growled and attacked each other, as if my words encouraged them. Which was ridiculous.

I pushed myself away from the chaos, my steps blurring, and my insides were being ripped into different directions. I wanted to cry for Eve's loss, stand up for myself against these wolves, and knock some damn sense into Daxon and Wilder.

Bursting outside, the cool air washed over me like I'd awakened from a dream, the fog clearing from my head.

Stumbling on the front steps, I looked back inside to where disorder reigned. This was madness, and if this was how the packs in this town settled anything, they were doing a great job of destroying themselves with the hatred they carried for one another.

A deep vibration jolted up my injured arm, a cruel jarring pain that had me wincing. I stared at my arm, at the blood dripping over my fingers. I needed to find a doctor, I was pretty sure I could see my bone.

Except as I watched the wound, it seemed to be getting smaller.

I frantically wiped the blood from my forearm, certain I was imagining things.

I watched in bewilderment as the injury closed up before my eyes, the skin knitting back together.

"Shit. How is this happening?"

Then it was gone. I kept running my hand over the skin that no longer hurt, that felt smooth to the touch. My heart thundered, pushing dread into my veins. I'd only ever healed like a human. This was...well, this was definitely new.

A shadow fell over me, and I lifted my head to find Daxon standing before me. He only wore his jeans stained with blood, while his chest was marred with cuts and bruises, his face not faring any better. More blood smeared his skin, and yet he just stared at my healed arm.

I swallowed hard, lowering my arm instantly.

"How did you heal so fast? Not even I can do that," he asked.

I was shaking my head as my stomach squeezed. "I-I don't know." I backed away from him, hating the way he stared at me like suddenly he saw a different part of me... one that might be hiding abilities capable of killing another shifter.

He reached out and grabbed my hand, then ran a finger tenderly over my skin where the wound had been moments earlier. A tingle buzzed from his touch and ran through my body, leaving me breathless. When I watched the way he studied my arm, I remembered the times we'd spent together, him taking me out to dinner for Creole food, sharing his cake with me, his kisses completely stealing me away. Then he'd showed me his true colors when I tried to leave this place. A part of me worried his golden exterior held something a lot darker than I first thought, and now I wasn't so sure about things between us.

"Rune," he began, almost sounding concerned. "I've never seen anyone heal this fast. What are you?"

Tears stung my eyes, and my chest felt like it might be cleaving in half. I'd been different my whole life, but to have him ask that question was like prying open my chest and tearing me apart.

My mind raced, searching for an explanation, for anything to tell him, but nothing came out. Instead, my thoughts spun with dread because I didn't need another complication. I knew who I was. I was nothing. I didn't know how to process any other reality.

I pulled my arm from Daxon's grip, but his hand

constricted, holding me by his side. "Don't be afraid of it." His words were gentle, yet my mind drowned in confusion.

"I need to go," I finally said and drew free from his grip.

"Rune," he said, stepping after me as I recoiled.

"No, please no. Just leave me alone." I jerked from his reach and then ran all the way back to the inn, terrified of what was going on with me.

*I*t was my first day of work since Eve's death.

And everything felt wrong.

Everything reminded me of Eve, and I had to stop myself a few times from looking over to ask her a question. Which was dumb. But I guessed it had already become a habit to bullshit with the sunny blonde all day while we were working.

Sorrow churned in my gut for what felt like the thousandth time, cloaking me and settling onto my shoulders until I felt like the world had darkened around me.

It was a strange thing, to mourn so much for an almost stranger. I thought part of me was mourning the loss of a fresh start. Eve had been my first friend, a symbol of the possibilities of this place. With her gone... and with the town turned against me...

Not to mention the killer lurking somewhere around.

Oh, and my weird new healing power that had sprung up.

Things had taken a turn for the worse.

The whole town was on pins and needles, especially after the disastrous town hall meeting. Neighbors who had once been friends now glared at each other suspiciously as they passed by. Fights between pack members were frequent, and fights between the Bitten and Lycan packs...they were nonstop. I hadn't had any one-on-one time with Wilder or Daxon since my encounter with Daxon the night of the town hall incident, a week ago. Any time I saw them in the street, they looked tense, haggard...exhausted. I knew from Jim and Carrie that they'd been working round the clock to try and calm the town down, a feat in itself since they'd also been ready to tear each other's throats out.

I tried not to miss Wilder...or Daxon. I tried not to read into their silence or the fact that they weren't around. I mean, why would some girl they'd been after mean much compared to the safety of their packs and the life they'd built for them?

See what I mean? I was spiraling.

The problem was that I'd had a lot of free time the last few days. I was supposed to work two days after Eve's death, but Marcus had let me know that the diner was basically a ghost town with everyone keeping to themselves, and they didn't need the help. I could hear the worry in his voice as he spoke to me, but surprisingly, I didn't hear any suspicion...or judgment.

If I hadn't already made up my mind that Marcus was good people, I would have then.

Without anything to do, and the fact that I couldn't go near the woods and run, I was restless. I tried old Sudoku puzzles that Carrie had lying around downstairs, and I'd tried to do push-ups in my room and even go on walks, daring everyone to glare at me as I passed them by.

But that insane urge to run, the one that I'd never experienced before coming here...it didn't go away.

I would lie in my bed at night, tossing and turning, sweat dripping down my spine as I fought the urge. It would be ridiculous...insane, to put myself at risk out there. But I knew in the back of my mind that I wouldn't be able to resist forever. There was something inside of me that had to feel the freedom that running had begun to make me feel. It was a need, not a want. I would just have to push it off for as long as possible.

When I did eventually fall asleep, my dreams had been filled with nightmares of Eve's lifeless eyes staring into the heavens and of the shadow creature in the woods.

Let's just say I wasn't looking like a well-adjusted, well rested woman at the moment.

I shook my head at my distracted thoughts when I realized I was pouring the water from my pitcher onto the table instead of the man's cup. The man in question glared at me as some of the water began to run into a rather awkward place on his lap. I started wiping down the table, my rag moving automatically to help with the water that had dripped on him until I realized I was about to wipe the man's crotch. He stared at me wide-eyed. I flicked my gaze to his dinner companion and realized with horror that he must be with his wife. She obviously thought I was trying to come on to her husband and looked like she was a second away from sticking her dinner knife into my jugular.

I quickly pulled my hand away from the stranger's, unfortunately, rising dick and backed away with my hands held up beseechingly to ward off any attack. "Let me get you some cheese sticks...on the house," I blurted out before scurrying away.

Licia was behind the bar today, and she was biting her lip and shining the same glass vigorously as she tried to contain her laughter. She'd obviously been watching me make a complete fool of myself.

"Don't say anything," I warned her as I typed in an order of cheese sticks into the diner computer, trying to stop blushing from embarrassment.

"You should have seen your face," she said with a snort as she wiped a tear from her cheek. "Maybe we should add massages as an extra dinner option. Harold looked like he'd be down for it."

"Harold," I whispered in disgust as I sneaked a glance at the man in question. His wife was furiously whisper yelling at him from behind her menu, and Harold looked like he wanted to disappear.

I groaned again and leaned my head against the wall as I listened to the cook whistle an off-key version of "Baby Got Back." "You can take the cheese sticks out of my check," I told her as she continued to laugh.

She wiped her eyes again. "Are you kidding me? That may have been the most hilarious thing I've ever seen. I should be the one paying you for the entertainment."

I stuck my tongue out at her and was about to say something when a bark of disgust from nearby reached my ears.

Licia's nose scrunched up. "Lord, help us," she

muttered as I turned to look where the sound was coming from.

As a favor to one of his buddies, Marcus had hired his buddy's sister to replace Eve. The new woman, Beverly... was unique.

"What is this?" she asked in an abnormally deep voice to the confused looking customer at the table she was in front of. Beverly was short and stocky, with saggy boobs that hung to her belly button by the looks of things. I didn't know what kind of bra she wore, if she wore one, but it wasn't very effective. She had a little bit of a mullet going on with grey streaked curly hair up front with a sort of long, wavy do happening in the back. I'm not even sure that Miyu could fix whatever Beverly had going on.

Besides her unusual looks, which frankly destroyed any notion I'd ever had that werewolves were all beautiful, Beverly also had an attitude that didn't quite fit the service industry, or really any industry actually. She was surly as a pit bull, couldn't smile at customers to save her life, and seemed to have the impression that customers were supposed to pay her an exorbitant tip no matter how her service was.

Licia was about to have a nervous breakdown because of her.

"Um, your tip," the customer answered, fidgeting nervously in his bench seat and looking around for help.

"You gave me a ten percent tip," Beverly continued as she held up the receipt in question furiously.

"You didn't even fill my water—" the man tried to bite back.

"If you think I slopped all over this restaurant to give

you your motherfucking dinner for a ten-percent tip, you have another thing coming," Beverly retorted, her voice rising with each word.

"I'm going to kill Marcus," Licia moaned before flinching in horror at her choice of words. It was a dangerous time to joke about murdering someone, not when there were real murders taking place. I gave her a weak, reassuring smile before wandering over to Beverly's table to try and calm her down before she scared off every other customer in the place. I may have wanted to leave here, but that still wasn't possible without any money. At this point, I wasn't sure that I was ever going to get my car back at the rate Wilder and Daxon were going.

Beverly's customer grabbed his wallet out of his pocket and fumbled with some bills with shaking hands.

"M-My mistake," he stuttered angrily, careful not to look Beverly in the eye, probably for fear that she'd attack. "I meant to give you twenty percent, of course," he said before hurriedly sliding out of the booth and rushing out of the restaurant.

I heard Licia's heavy sigh as the front door slammed after him. I doubt we'd be seeing him again.

I threw Beverly a look, but she didn't see it. She was too busy greedily counting her money. For a second, I wondered if maybe I should try her tactics for a while, she certainly got tips. It would take a while for the customers to run out...right?

"Beverly, in the back," snapped Licia. Beverly squared her shoulders as if readying to march into war and headed back towards the stock room, where Licia had begun to walk towards.

I shook my head, half amused, half annoyed, and started wrapping silverware while I waited for those cheese sticks to come out. Our cheese sticks were really good. Hopefully, the wife would be too busy enjoying them to come after me when I returned to her table. Even so, maybe I should take her knife away...just to be safe.

The bell attached to the front door rang, and I automatically called out a welcome to the newcomer before even looking to see who had come in. I was faintly aware of the person settling in at the bar while I finished wrapping the last of the tray of silverware I'd been working on.

When I could feel someone's gaze drilling into me, I finally looked up to see who had walked in.

My silverware crashed to the ground when I saw who it was.

It was Sterling, one of Alistair's enforcers. My hands were shaking as I crouched to the ground and tried to pick up the silverware. I could feel other people's eyes on me as I fumbled around, clattering the forks and knives together as I tried to give myself time to think.

How had he found me? There was no way this could be a fluke, right? No way that Sterling had just been in the neighborhood and somehow found his way here?

Fuck, fuck, fuck. What was I going to do?

"Order up," the cook called. I wiped my sweaty palms on my apron and stood up, trying to keep my face blank and not convey the panic I was feeling. Out of all of Alistair's enforcers, Sterling had been the one who thrived off panic. He loved anytime he had the opportunity to lord over those weaker than him. He had a special fondness for using his authority on girls in the pack. I'd heard their screams sometimes from the backrooms in the house that Alistair used for "pack business."

I barely suppressed a shiver as I walked over to grab the steaming plate of cheese sticks along with the ranch dressing we served with it. I studiously ignored Sterling as I passed him to get to the table. I set the food down, barely registering the murderous glare from the woman. She was the least of my problems at the moment.

I looked around the room, seeing if there was anyone else that needed something that I could use as a distraction, but everyone looked fine.

Still, I grabbed a water pitcher and began topping off already full drinks as I tried to stretch when I would meet my ending.

I wished that Licia and Beverly would come back, but really...what could they do? Even Beverly, as fierce as she was, wouldn't stand a chance against a pack enforcer like Sterling.

I took a deep breath and just decided to get it over with. I knew Alistair was going to come after me. Not only was I his fated mate, rejected or not, but I'd freaking cut out the guy's eyeball and drugged him and all of his men.

I'd just hoped that he wouldn't succeed with his search. As I walked behind the bar to face Sterling, it was like I could almost hear a death knell playing in the background, telling me with every step how utterly and completely fucked I was.

And not in the good way I'd been after Wilder had left my room the other night.

"What can I get for you?" I asked Sterling, still

working hard to keep my face blank, like I didn't recognize him, even as my tone dripped with disdain.

Something twitched in Sterling's cheek at my insolence. For as long as he'd known me, I'd been practically mute. "Yes, sir. No, sir... Please don't, sir." Those had basically been the only words I'd said to him.

Sterling stared at me with a little smirk on his face as I catalogued his features. He was good-looking, like all of Alistair's men had been. He was dressed in a preppy collared shirt with the collar popped, a visual representation of the douchiness of this man. Evidently, he still hadn't been told by anyone that popped collars weren't in. Pity.

Sterling's hair was perfectly cut with what I was sure were fake highlights streaked through his hair. I thought he even got his eyebrows waxed, because they'd always looked a little bit too perfectly shaped to be real.

The thing about Sterling though, he may have looked like a preppy boy who'd run away at the first sign of trouble, but that couldn't be further from the truth. He had a cruel streak a million miles wide. I'd seen him personally in the fight nights that Alistair held to fix pack grievances, knocking the utter shit out of men twice the size of him.

I'd been afraid of him since I'd met him, but right now? Right now, I couldn't summon up any fear. All I felt was hate. This town might have had a lot of problems. It may not have been the most welcoming place at the moment either. But at least it had felt a little bit like mine for a moment.

And now here Sterling was, leaking Alistair into the

air around me so I wouldn't be able to envision this place without envisioning him here too.

Why did everything have to suck so bad?

I squeezed my fists together in frustration and gasped when I felt something cut into my skin. I'd evidently grabbed a knife without even looking.

"It's good to see you too, Rune," Sterling purred, and I winced at hearing my name come from his lips. "We've all been so worried about you since the little incident."

Incident. Is that what they were calling it?

A little snort sneaked past my lips, but my heart panged as I thought of Alistair.

Surprisingly though, thinking of him didn't quite hurt as bad as it used to.

I leaned in close, dropping all pretenses. "I'm not going back with you," I swore to him, and I hoped he could see the resolve in my eyes. I hoped he could see how much I would kick and scream and make it as difficult as humanly possible for him to get me from this place.

It had taken everything in me to escape the first time.

And I knew I'd never get a chance to do it again if Alistair got his clutches on me once again.

Sterling looked a bit shocked at my words, which I didn't blame him for. I scarcely recognized myself nowadays. In a way, I'd been reborn when I'd escaped from Alistair. I wasn't saying that I liked who I was becoming, but at least it was different from the weak creature I'd been before.

I pointed the knife towards Sterling, trying to hide it

from the sight of the customers... I was kind of proud of myself that I was only shaking a little bit.

"You need to leave right now," I told him, trying to put as much bravado as I could.

He threw his head back and laughed. "You know this whole time, we pitied Alistair for having you as a mate... thought he'd done the right thing casting you aside, even though it had to have hurt him like hell. A little mouse like you...with the next Alpha? It was insulting, Rune," he said silkily, leaning closer toward me. "But after what you did to get away and what I'm seeing right now, I'm beginning to think he messed up."

This time, I couldn't hold back the shiver that scuttled down my skin at the unbridled lust in his eyes as he watched me speculatively. I didn't even know what to say.

He blinked a few times and shook his head, and when he looked at me again, the lust was gone. "Unfortunately for you, Rune. I don't think the bossman's really happy with you. Ya know? That was a pretty naughty thing you did. You're going to be begging for his forgiveness for a long, long time."

He purposely slowed down his words so that he was emphasizing just how long I'd be begging.

Licia rounded the corner just then, followed by a surly looking Beverly. I wiped my sweaty palms again and hurried from behind the bar and away from Sterling. Licia frowned at Sterling and threw me a questioning look, but I avoided her gaze. I knew that Sterling wouldn't mind one bit slaughtering every person in here in order to get what he wanted.

I have to get away. I have to get away, I chanted, on the edge of a panic attack.

Once around the bar, I stared around blankly, not sure what to do. Just then, the cook yelled out that another order was up. Before Licia or Beverly could grab it, I tossed the food on a tray and walked out to the table area, only belatedly realizing that I had no idea which table the food was for.

Sterling swiveled his chair around to look at me, and I swear I was on the verge of a nervous breakdown. So much for all the bravado I'd been pretending to have. I hadn't changed at all. I was still a little mouse.

Just then, the bell rang, and I swear I almost burst into tears because Daxon had just walked in. I tossed the food onto a nearby table, not even bothering to check if it was their food, and then practically flung myself at a surprised Daxon.

"Sweetheart, what's wrong?" he asked softly, the sweet tone reminding me of how he'd been before I found out the town was filled with wolves. I just squeezed him tighter, unable to speak for a moment.

When had he started to feel like that? Like he was my safe place? He certainly hadn't done anything to deserve that title. But yet here I was, in his arms, so freaking happy he was here.

Just then, Sterling walked by, headed towards the front door. He held my gaze the entire time he crossed the room, that same cruel smirk draped across his lips. "I'll be seeing you, Rune," he said in a voice laden with promises.

Daxon froze against me when he heard Sterling's

statement. He set me down carefully before turning around and skewering Sterling with a terrifying stare. Sterling, for his part, kept up his cocky face, his smile only dimming a bit. He held Daxon's gaze for a long minute until he finally was forced to submit and look away. This obviously pissed him off because he stormed out of the restaurant, the door slamming behind him. We were really lucky it hadn't broken yet.

It didn't matter that Sterling was leaving now. I knew he'd be back.

Daxon watched Sterling walk away until he was out of sight. I jumped when he suddenly turned around and grabbed my arm. "We need to talk," he announced sternly as he began to drag me towards the back room. Licia gave me a nervous stare as I passed by, and Beverly smacked her fist against her hand like she was asking if I wanted her to beat Daxon up. That would certainly be interesting to see her try.

I squeaked when he pulled me forward once again, and I found myself in the stock room. Was he even allowed to be back here?

"Who was that guy?" Daxon growled and my eyes widened at how furious he looked. Or maybe furious wasn't the right word. Daxon was...jealous?

"A nightmare from my past," I told him with a shaky sigh. "He's one of my ex's enforcers. Evidently, my ex has been looking for me." I hugged my arms around myself to try and ward off the sudden chill. "And he's finally found me."

"Is this the ex you told me you were running from?" he asked, a strange intensity settling over his skin. It was like I could see it happening. As we stood there and talked, Daxon was becoming someone else. Someone darker...more out of control.

His comment reminded me of the date we'd had. That seemed like a million years ago right now. It was hard to believe that had ever happened. Especially with the version of Daxon standing in front of me now.

I nodded, trying to get ahold of myself before I burst into tears. It was hard to control though. The fear was hot and thick in my stomach.

He suddenly pulled me into his arms. "Fuck. You're fucking terrified, sweetheart. Your whole body's shaking," he said as he wrapped himself around me.

I soaked in the warmth and the dark intensity shrouding him. It felt comforting, protective. I probably should have been frightened at how many masks Daxon seemed to wear. I didn't think that I'd actually met the real him yet. But somehow, I wasn't worried. Something inside of me told me that Daxon was dangerous to everyone else but me.

"I'm going to take care of this," he whispered in my ear, and I nodded against his chest as I remained buried against him. It was nice to trust... Even if the trust felt a little blind.

I'd trusted once before though, trusted that my fated mate would only have the best interests in mind for my heart. And I'd been destroyed.

It was hard to make the leap again, maybe stupid too, since Daxon was still a stranger, but the truth was...I was exhausted. I had to trust him to help me because I didn't have any other options. And as much as I wanted to run, I knew I wouldn't get far.

Please don't betray me, my soul whispered to him.

And although I was probably imagining it, I swore his soul whispered back, *never*.

Daxon

THE HARDEST THING about being a psychopath is that you had to be so fucking on all the time. Someday, I just wanted to shed my skin, metaphorically of course, and show the world who I really was. Of course that would mean losing out on all the fun I had tricking everyone around me. Only Wilder seemed to have a suspicion that the face I showed the world wasn't who I really was. He'd always been a smart bastard.

I had cravings. Cravings that sometimes felt overwhelming. The best I could do was hold them off until I found an opportune time, one that wouldn't have me featured on the ten o'clock news. My craving right now though...was to show Rune the real me. To peel off the golden boy smile and see what she thought of the monster underneath. The monster who craved blood, who rejoiced in the beauty of watching a cut on the skin, the one who loved the sound of pain.

Rune was shy, timid...broken. But something inside of me just told me she had a darker edge. One that wouldn't mind what my darkness would give her.

The ability to not worry.

Because there weren't monsters out there scarier than

me. If she ever agreed to be mine, she'd never have to be afraid of the dark again.

Maybe she'd even join me there.

She'd seemed calmer after I left. I could feel the fragile trust she was giving me. And I wasn't going to let her down. It just so happened that me helping her out went well with one of my favorite past times. It was always perfect when things worked out like that.

A few old biddies walked by, and I gave them my best smile. They immediately started to titter and blush. They were the easiest to prey on. Most of the pack and towns-people in general were like that. They saw what they wanted to see. It was only the ones closest to me in power, my betas...and Wilder, an alpha like me, who got the sensation that something was a little off. I could see it in my betas' gazes sometimes. They would study me, thinking that I didn't notice, even though I fucking noticed everything. I could smell the fear on them in those moments, wondering when I would turn my atten-tion their way. Of course, I'd never confided in any of them what I really liked to do for fun, but I'm sure the thought sometimes crossed their minds...wondering who I really was. They never pressed any deeper than that though. As a wolf, it was engrained in you to submit to your Alpha. And I may have been a psychopath, but I'd never betrayed that blind devotion. Maybe that was the only decent thing about me.

My phone buzzed just then, and I pulled it out of my pocket, hoping I'd be getting the information I wanted.

Jawbone Pub, Sin, my beta, had messaged. As soon as I'd noticed the stranger in the bar, I'd had my men on the move to make sure there was an eye on him at all times.

I've got him, I wrote back, signaling that he needed to go about his business. There wouldn't be any need to watch *Sterling* after I got done with him.

I made my way over to the pub. I actually hadn't been in for a while. It had been a place that I'd go to pick up my lucky lady for the night, but ever since I'd met Rune... well, I hadn't felt the urge. One thing you could say for the demon that lurked inside of me, he didn't care for anyone, until her. One look at her, and we'd become obsessed, determined to maim, kill, destroy, obliterate anyone who stood between us and our girl.

Sterling clocked me the second I stepped into the pub. He was sitting at the bar in the corner, a sign of his enforcer training. It was one of the only seats in the place you could sit and see everyone around you. He wasn't looking to get jumped from behind.

I offered him a charming smile with just an edge of teeth, enough to put him on notice that I presented danger, but not send him running.

Dietra gave me a wide grin, already leaning in to try and give me as much of a view as possible of her rack without actually stripping. I'd made the mistake of fucking her one blue moon, and she'd been after my balls ever since then.

Not interested.

I ambled my way over to my prey and sat next to him, signaling to Dietra that I wanted my usual. I could feel the gazes of others in the room. Between the stranger and a Bitten in the bar, they were having trouble keeping their eyes off us. Normally, they would at least pretend to not be staring at me, since we'd coexisted in peace for generations. But with Eve's death, that had changed. They were still terrified of me, as they should've been, but evidently, they were determined to keep an eye on the big bad wolf in the room, even if it was obvious.

"I have a feeling you're not the welcome wagon," the dead man drawled as he took a long pull from his beer, his hands only slightly shaking. I'd noticed that in the restaurant too, while I was cataloging how exactly I was going to kill him and dismember his body. He put on a brave face, but he had shaky hands. I'm sure his Alpha just loved that about him.

I hummed non-committally for a second as Dietra came over to give me my favorite draft, a local beer from a town nearby actually. Jawbone was the only place in town that carried it. She gave me a hopeful smile as she pretended to polish an already sparkling glass. Sterling was eating her up, a sparkle in his gaze that let me know if he were to survive the night, Dietra might not.

"I'll let you know if I need another," I told Dietra with a wink, and her smile fell as she got the hint she wasn't wanted.

Sterling huffed next to me as she left, not missing out on the chance to watch her ass as she went away.

"Is this where you warn me out of town?" he finally said, my silence obviously doing its intended job of making him uneasy.

I chuckled darkly. "On the contrary, my friend. I happen to be thrilled you've come into town."

His gaze shot to me, a white line appearing around his lips as his scent began to smell like fear.

I sipped my drink, humming a bit under my breath. I could feel his terror grow.

It was delicious.

"I know your game, Bitten. But it's not going to work. You're not going to scare me away. And you know what, I've decided that I deserve to play a little bit before I bring Rune back to my alpha. Her cunt must be worth something, don't you think? I mean, it's been enough to drive him crazy, even after he rejected her." He laughed then, the sound coming off a little too high-pitched to fool anyone. He was about to piss his pants. "Do you think she's a screamer? Does she get off on a little pain? Because—"

I plunged a syringe into his leg just then because I was tired of listening to his shit. I usually liked to play with my victims more, but evidently, listening to another male talk about Rune was my breaking point.

I'd still have fun with this next part.

The drug set in quickly, moving through his bloodstream and creating a euphoric effect. To anyone watching him, they'd just think Sterling had one too many drinks. In reality, the drug basically worked to imprison him in his mind. His body could move, but he wasn't in control any longer.

I was.

"Let's get you up, buddy," I told him, helping him off the chair. I shot a flirty smile to Dietra, and she swooned as I began to walk Sterling to the door. "I think he's feeling that last one. I'm going to help him get to the hotel."

She looked at me like I was some kind of hero, and I winked at her just to make sure all she would remember from this night was thinking she might finally be getting somewhere with me. I slapped Sterling's back, and he fell forward a bit before beginning to walk to the door as if in a trance.

Once we got outside, I directed Sterling to the back of the bar, where I'd parked my car. Not many people knew I even had one since I usually rode my bike everywhere. It was perfect for stowing...extra passengers.

Sterling sat quietly in the passenger seat, staring blankly ahead and twitching every once in a while. I turned on the radio and sang my heart out to "Welcome to the Jungle." It was an oldie but a goodie, that was for sure.

We drove out of town, weaving around the one lane road that carved through the forest until we got to where the turn off was for my cabin. An overgrown dirt path darted off to the left, and I took it, my singing growing louder.

After driving for a mile, I rounded one more curve and then I was there. I couldn't wait until I could show this place to Rune someday, I knew she'd understand. You just needed a place to be able to get away from it all.

I snorted at the thought as I parked. I got out of the car, inhaling the forest around me, scenting the air to make sure I couldn't smell anyone nearby. The air was blissfully clear.

I walked over to the passenger side door and opened

it up. Sterling sat there calmly, not even looking over at me.

"Welcome home, Sterling. I think you're going to really enjoy it here."

Sterling stumbled as I grabbed his arm and heaved him out of the car. I took him through the main floor of the cabin to the back guest bedroom, where behind a shelf in the wall, there was a set of stairs that led to the "entertainment room" of the place.

I led Sterling in front of me and then promptly pushed him down the set of stairs. The drugs worked so perfectly that he didn't even scream as he fell down the entire flight.

I'd need to change that. It was always better when they screamed.

A chair sat in the middle of the room, a drain underneath it. The floor was slightly sloped in the middle so any fluids would drain easily. I sat him down in the chair and then went over and turned on my sound system, blasting some classic rock as I went to work.

First, I tied his ankles to the legs of the chair and then tied his arms behind him. I then took a syringe of the antidote to the drug I'd injected him with earlier and stuck it into his thigh, laying out my tools while it kicked in.

Terrified breathing started up, along with short moaning gasps.

Sterling was back.

I walked around to the front of him and then crouched down.

"How you feeling, bud?" I asked, smiling wildly.

I cackled as the front of his pants began to darken as he pissed himself, his gasps increasing.

"What are you—" he began.

I promptly sliced off his tongue with the knife I was holding in my hands.

His screams lit up the room.

I closed my eyes, the sound better than any music I'd ever heard.

"You should have left her alone, Sterling. No one's going to take Rune from me, no one. Not you and certainly not your boss. And anyone he sends her way is going to find themselves in the exact same situation as you are right now."

Sterling blubbered, tears and snot streaming down his face...along with the blood of course. Mouth wounds always did bleed a lot.

I waved the knife in front of his face and watched as Sterling tried desperately to move and get away, something he failed at, obviously.

"Now let's see, do you think your alpha would appreciate your head, your hand...or your dick as a little present?"

Sterling's muffled screams intensified.

"Sorry, man, I can't quite understand you." I laughed. "Did you say 'dick'? You want to give him your dick? I agree, that's probably best. Probably sends him the best warning about what exactly will happen to any dick that gets close to Rune."

I sliced the front of his pants open, showcasing his tiny dick. "No wonder you're such a douche, Sterling. I probably would be too if I had a stump like that." I cackled again as he cried out.

I walked over to my table and picked up the large butcher knife. "This should do quite nicely. Blunt enough that it might take a few whacks to get it off."

Sterling was full on screaming at this point. He was utterly terrified. It was fantastic.

I walked over and stood right in front of him as "Sweet Caroline" began to stream through the speakers. "Now make sure to sing along during the chorus," I admonished him as I raised the knife. "And do tell the devil I send my regards."

I sliced the knife down at the base of his dick.

I'd been right—the knife really was too blunt to do it in just one cut.

THE SOUNDTRACK HAD SWITCHED to something darker, edgier as I tried to settle myself after the high that always came out of a kill. I washed my hands, the water initially dark red before eventually clearing up. Sterling lay in pieces next to the chair. I'd lost a little bit of control for a moment when I'd thought about the things he'd said about Rune. The place was a little bit wrecked. Time for cleanup.

I tossed my clothes and the pieces of Sterling's body into the pig pen I kept out back, sans his dick of course, which would be mailed to Rune's ex. Trying to delay the inevitable, I showered and changed into a pair of new clothes. My whole body was shaking with the adrenaline rush. There was really nothing like it.

But finally, I couldn't hold myself back any longer.

I had to see Rune.

I drove like a maniac back to town, dropping off my car first at a garage I kept near my house and then grabbing my bike.

Somehow...I made it to the inn.

Get ahold of yourself, man. She's not ready.

I flicked a finger at Jim as I passed through the bar and restaurant area. He gave me a knowing look that I ignored. I could care less about any of the Lycan fuckers. All I cared about was getting to her.

The stairs seemed to last forever, but finally, I was there in front of her door.

My body was shaking like a fucking junkie, and I knew when she saw me, she would know immediately something was off.

Taking a deep, shaking breath, I banged on the door.

Rune

I PACED MY ROOM NERVOUSLY, wondering when Sterling was going to make his move. Daxon had said he would take care of him, but what did that mean? Could it really be as easy as that? For a man to actually promise me something and then he actually fulfilled his promise?

It seemed too good to be true.

Pound, pound, pound. Something banged on the door,

and I jumped, my heart fluttering wildly at the sudden sound.

Was it Sterling? Had he come for me?

"Who is it?" I called out, knowing that wouldn't stop him from coming in no matter what I did. But at least the crowd downstairs might hear my screams.

Although with the way they'd been lately, I was pretty sure they would hand me over for torture in a heartbeat.

"It's me," Daxon said roughly, a thread of what almost sounded like desperation in his voice.

I let out a sigh of relief and threw open the door.

No sooner had I done so than Daxon was on me, his lips pressed against me frantically like he'd never been more desperate for something in his whole life. Our lips crashed together again and again in a hard, fast embrace. One touch from him, and I'd become obsessed. We gripped each other's faces like lifelines as our mouths connected on a level so deep, I swore I could taste his soul.

We pulled at each other, both frantic to somehow get as close to each other as we could. Our bodies heaved with need as everything that had been building up the last few weeks...every touch, every thought, every heavy look, poured into this embrace and into each other.

I never wanted it to stop.

He thrust himself against me, and that was all it took for me to jump into his arms, his hands squeezing and kneading my ass as he walked us to the bed.

A little voice in the back of my head reminded me that I'd had Wilder on this bed a very short time ago.

I told that bitch to shut the hell up.

He rolled against me again, and I squeezed my thighs around him, even as he went to lay me down on the bed, forcing him to follow me down. I wanted more, but somehow, I also wanted less. Less clothes for sure.

And maybe less thinking.

As he touched me, the past seemed to slip away, almost like it didn't exist. If there were a way to bottle up that feeling, I would, just so I could carry it with me always and feel free from the memories that constantly haunted me.

I never thought I'd enjoy sex...crave it even, after what I've been through. Like everything else in my life, my mother had romanticized what it would be like...making love with your one and only. Insert sarcasm obviously.

I'd even saved myself for my true mate.

And while that might have been an epic love story with another couple, saving myself for Alistair had just been tragic. Sometimes, it didn't even feel real what he'd done to me that night after he'd rejected me, like it had happened to someone else and it was just a movie that I had the unfortunate ability to see over and over again in my mind.

"Stay with me," he ordered breathlessly as he moved one hand into my hair and gripped it by the roots, pulling my head back and deepening our kiss. His firm grip centered me. My thoughts came flying back to the way his lips felt against mine, the way his sunshine hair brushed silkily against my cheek.

I wanted this to be just fucking. But there was something wild in his kiss, just like with Wilder. Daxon's kiss felt like a claiming. It was unrelenting and pressure filled.

His tongue plunged and begged for mine to give in to him.

I can just pretend right now, I told myself.

I wanted to pretend because it felt natural to be with Daxon like this. Just as it had with Wilder. To let him possess my body. I thirsted for it.

His mouth moved to my neck, his breath hot on my skin as I fumbled for his jeans, my hands shaking as I tried to unbutton them without him getting any farther away from me. Finally, I shoved them off his ass, not finding it at all surprising that Daxon was commando. Whatever ideas I'd formed about who Daxon was at the beginning had been obliterated as of late. He was an enigma wrapped in an angelic package. But I knew that what lay under the mask he wore was a whole different beast.

And somehow, that made him even hotter.

Daxon pushed his cock back and forth in my hand as I squeezed his silky hardness, groaning loudly into my neck as he moved. With one wild move, he literally sliced the front of my leggings open, obviously having trans-formed his hand into a claw to manage the feat.

Wild heat surged between my legs as I watched the savageness in his eyes, the golden glory of them almost disappearing with how much his black pupils had extended. A loud rip tore through the air as he finished obliterating my leggings, throwing them somewhere behind him.

I was going to make him buy me some more. I had limited clothing and limited resources to get clothing after all. His hand slid up between my legs, and his fingers slipped inside the crotch of my panties that had somehow survived his mauling. His finger teased my opening as he touched me through the thin, sopping wet cloth. He bent his head and licked my slit through the cloth, and somehow, I almost came undone. He groaned, a low, decadent groan that had me blushing, even though there was no one to see what I'd done.

No idea why that had seemed so sexual, but the sight of a golden god between my legs was heady and over-whelming.

Suddenly, he leaned back and managed to flip me over. I let out a loud squeak as I bounced on the bed. A loud tear signaled that my shirt was now ruined as well.

Daxon licked down my spine before suddenly biting my exposed right butt cheek that peeked out from my thong.

Why had that been so freaking hot?

A smack landed right on the opposite cheek from the one he'd just bitten. The sound startled me, and my jaw dropped. In less than a ten-second time span, he'd bitten me and spanked me.

"Oh!" I squeaked as I realized my ass cheeks weren't the only thing on my body throbbing. Daxon began to drop kisses down my spine again as he squeezed and stroked my tingling ass. I pushed against his hands, crazily turned on.

"Please," I moaned. "Do it again."

Daxon froze in place, still palming my butt. "What was that, Rune?" he said in a low, deep, grumbly voice that honestly did as much for my insides as everything else he'd done.

I paused, a quick moment of shame and terror passing over me as I realized what I'd said. Did I like that kind of thing? And more importantly...how did I like that kind of thing after everything with Alistair?

Don't think about him, I admonished myself.

Hmm...maybe I was actually into spanking. Maybe that was a way for me to take back my power in a way. I wasn't going to think about it too hard, I decided.

"Do it again," I said, more firmly this time. Daxon still hesitated, obviously unsure if I actually meant what I was saying. I didn't really blame him for that. The version of Rune that he'd known had been the meek church mouse. And maybe just like I was discovering there was more to Daxon than first met the eye...maybe he was discovering the same thing about me.

Daxon finally chuckled darkly as he began to massage my ass again in his rough, perfect hands. "Rune, say the words again. Tell me what you want me to do to your sexy, fucking ass. The sexiest I've ever seen. I want to hear you say it again."

Daxon plus dirty talk was definitely my weakness I decided right then.

I cleared my throat and pushed against him as I spoke. "Spank me again. Please."

Another growl rolled in his chest as he began to kiss the side of my face, my neck, and my shoulder. He buried his face against that same place between my neck and my shoulder that Wilder had been so fond of and stayed there for a moment, his chest rising and falling rapidly and his entire body laced with tension.

"You're fucking perfect. I knew you would be," he

whispered against my skin. Without another word, he grabbed my hips and pulled me back into his enormous erection, grinding against my crack as his hands pushed my ruined shirt and bra all the way off my shoulders.

I shivered as my nipples peaked. My breath faltered as Daxon's hands slid up my hips, and then my stomach, and over my breasts. His movements were slow and methodical, designed to destroy me with every movement. He pulled me up so his chest was pressed against my back and then he began to massage and stroke my aching breasts. He suddenly pinched one of my nipples, the sharp burst of pain shocking me, but then somehow spiking my pleasure even more.

My entire body heaved with desire. His teeth scraped against my neck as he whispered, "Maybe my good girl isn't such a good girl after all."

It. Was. Official.

Daxon was going to destroy me.

"Maybe you don't actually know me as well as you think you do, golden boy," I murmured, the nickname slipping out.

He chuckled, a bit evilly if I was being honest. "Likewise, sweetheart," he said.

He bit my neck, almost savagely, and then shoved me down again. For a moment, dark thoughts from the past threatened. Taking a deep breath, I pushed those fuckers as far away as I could.

Daxon ran his hands greedily over my ass, squeezing and fondling the flesh. It was kind of a strange thing honestly to know that someone was staring at your ass and admiring it... Maybe worshipping was actually the right word for what Daxon's gaze and touch were doing right now. See...strange.

"So you liked being spanked," he mused as his lips danced momentarily across my skin.

Desire dripped down my thighs just anticipating him doing it again.

"Yes," I rasped, rubbing against his hands shamelessly. He continued to stroke my cheeks, and I just knew even without seeing him that he was laughing at me.

"Let's make sure you actually love it, shall we?"

Daxon moved away from me for a second, and I sucked in a sharp breath as the sharp bite of a claw dragged against my cheek. It abruptly sliced through the thin strap of my thong. He yanked the fabric away and then abruptly licked through my slit, making me shudder and let out a garbled moan.

"Look at you. Your fucking soaked, and I haven't even done anything to you." His finger gently danced across my clit, sending electric pulses through my entire body. "Say it again, Rune," he ordered.

I looked over my shoulder, my lids heavy with desire. His pupils were blown out even more, and I was a little entranced at the thin band of gold I could see peeking out. He grinned at me, a sharp-toothed grin that showed his incisors had lengthened like he was having trouble not wolfing out. Had to admit, it was sexy how much the Bitten could transform at will. Or at least it was sexy on Daxon.

I took a deep breath and tried to channel my inner and practically non-existent badass as I shot him a wink. "Spank me, Master," I told him with a smirk.

He growled again, his wolf really liking the image that "master" was giving him. And I had to admit, I liked thinking about it too. Which again, made no sense whatsoever.

His hand suddenly hit my ass cheek in a surprisingly hard smack that had me lurching forward...much different than the previous one.

I almost came. I really almost did. I pressed my forehead against the scratchy, cheap comforter, trying to get myself under control because I knew Daxon would get far too much pleasure if he could make me come with just one swat. I closed my eyes tightly until I felt the pleasure start to retreat and then pushed myself back into him, a little too obsessed with his warmth, his skin, his touch.

Daxon plunged a finger deep into my core, and I barked out a cry. "So wet and tight, sweetheart," he growled out, dropping a kiss onto my still throbbing cheek where he just slapped. His tongue swept obscenely across my heated skin as he murmured, "Fucking perfect," against me.

My moan was desperate as I began to rock back into him, following the perfect rhythm of his fingers as they pumped in and out of me.

"Don't come, don't come, don't come," I chanted under my breath.

Daxon, of course, must have somehow heard me because he laughed darkly once more. Why was that sound so freaking sexy?

"Does my good girl want more?" he mockingly asked, even though the answer was obvious. He circled my clit softly with what felt like the very tip of his claw, and I practically cried out from the effort it was taking to keep myself from going right off the edge.

"Yes." The plea slipped out, but I'd just reached the point of not caring. "Fucking spank me again. Please do it again," I moaned out over and over again.

"You're going to come for me, just this way. And then I'm going to be inside of you," he promised me. And I was all for him fulfilling that promise, that was for sure. Daxon reverently stroked my ass with both hands, his deep moan echoing around the room. He let go of me for one second, and I held my breath, waiting for the pain and the pleasure I was desperate for. His hand landed swiftly, again and again and again. He alternated between each cheek, every swat landing in rapid succession so I never had a chance to come down from the thrall he had me in. The final slap was right on my clit, and my body went spiraling into an all-consuming release I wasn't sure could ever be topped. Nonsensical words erupted from my mouth as his tongue stroked my too sensitive clit as my orgasm continued to rush through me. I felt the climax in every inch of my body. I didn't know it was even possible for one to last this long.

Daxon's tongue abruptly left, and I collapsed to the bed, my whole body shaking and crazy over what had just happened.

These guys were ruining me, ripping me up into little pieces and putting me back together again in a way that somehow had them laced through my very veins. Taking a deep breath, I finally managed to flop back onto my back, immediately finding it hard to breathe as I saw how Daxon was looking at me.

Daxon's eyes blazed into mine, the gold of them trying to overpower the dark as he stared at me with longing and urgency and something deeper. I wanted to look away because I knew what he'd see reflected in my eyes. But I couldn't. The look felt impossible and important, and I knew I'd be obsessing about it long after this moment was over.

A streak of red caught my eye, and I frowned as I reached up and noticed a bit of blood painted on his ear.

"Are you hurt?" I said foggily, wondering if I'd somehow scratched him as he'd made me come undone.

He was still for a moment, his gaze still unyielding on mine. But this time, they were searching. Details came into clearer focus as I realized that the blood wasn't his. Daxon pressed his forehead against mine, so close to me that his lips moved against mine when he finally spoke.

"You're never going to have to worry about Sterling again, baby," he murmured, not answering my question, but answering my question at the same time.

I froze underneath him. Was he saying what I thought he was saying? The underlying tension to his words made it clear that Sterling was gone in a permanent way, not in a temporary way like he'd just been run out of town.

For a second, it was hard to connect golden god Daxon with actually having the ability to kill someone. But as I studied his face and saw once again the dark secrets written across his features, I remembered how he'd been when he'd caught me in the woods.

It wasn't such a huge jump to imagine him gutting Sterling.

And the thought that this beautiful creature had cared enough to kill for me...well, I loved it.

And that was when I knew how completely fucked in the head I actually was.

And I found myself not actually caring.

"Good," I growled.

His body shuddered for a second as shock blew across his face. "Good?" he asked, a bit of vulnerability in his words.

"Yes, Daxon. I love that. I love that you protected me. I love that he's gone. I love—" I cut myself off before I could say anything else.

With a wild, ravaged growl, Daxon bent his head to my chest and began to worship my breasts with his lips and tongue, palming me roughly in a way that skipped perfectly on that line between pain and pleasure. I was immediately on the edge of an orgasm once again.

I moaned as the delicious agony of his touch on my clit throbbed out of control. I was nothing but need and desire, a person completely disconnected from reality. He turned me to my stomach once more as his hands roamed over my hips and groin. He pressed his silky hardness against my backside, the sensation causing goosebumps to ripple over my entire body. Evidently, Daxon was very much an ass man. For a moment, I imagined what it would feel like for Daxon to actually be inside my ass...but I tabled that for another day.

Daxon surprised me by moving me down with him so he cradled me as he lay behind me. He held my leg up and positioned his cock at my center. Without a word, he thrust into me, his thickness somehow hell and heaven on my swollen tissues all at the same time.

He cupped my jaw and roughly moved my head so that I was forced to look at him...not that it was a burden to do so.

"Rune," he whispered. His eyes were wild. They reminded me of how Wilder was always calling me wild. How he said there was something inside of me. These men though...their wildness was tangible, like you could taste it, feel it, dive into it. And I didn't find myself wanting to cage it up. I wanted to follow it, become the wild that they were.

Motherfucker. I was falling in love with him. I was falling in love with both of them.

How the hell had this happened? Dammit all to hell.

Daxon sealed his mouth over mine and assaulted me with deep, drugging kisses, all while still frozen inside me. He kissed me lazily, as if we had all the time in the world. And wouldn't it have been nice if we did? I could definitely get on board with having an eternity of these delirium inducing kisses that threatened to make me orgasm from just the kiss alone.

I was pretty sure it was getting to the point that Daxon and Wilder could just look at me and somehow, I'd fly right over the edge. My thoughts scattered away as Daxon began to pump his hips against me, his hard cock moving in and out, over and over and over again. So deep. So slow. So fucking perfect.

I gripped the comforter as he stroked that perfect, secret spot inside of me. I was going to die of pleasure. I was never going to survive this.

"Come for me again, sweetheart."

"Yes, yes, yes," I said desperately, my body trembling in his arms as my hoarse voice gasped for air.

"Knew you'd be perfect for me the second I saw you. Knew you'd be mine."

"Yes," I moaned, my climb building from his words and his movements.

"Knew that I'd do anything to have you...anything to keep you."

I should have maybe been a little bit more scared of the words coming from his beautiful lips. Maybe I should have run from the room screaming. But I'd just gotten hot over the fact that he'd killed someone. So whatever.

If I was being honest with myself, my soul was desperate for the words of devotion that these two men had given me. I'd been rejected by the one who was supposed to love me the most. The one who was supposed to love me forever. The possessiveness coming from the two of them was what I hadn't known I needed. And maybe a part of me did want to run screaming or to flip out like I'd already done with Wilder. But right now, just for this moment, I allowed myself to breathe in his words of obsessive devotion, to allow it to seal up some of the tears and cracks written across my soul.

I knew I was supposed to only care about loving myself, and that was a constant work in progress. But maybe, just maybe, it was okay if it felt good that they seemed to be falling in love with me too.

"Rune. Sweetheart," he groaned, his face flinching. "I need you to come. I need you to come now." He slid his hand down my stomach, between my legs, and circled my clit expertly. My eyes slammed shut as instant fireworks shot off in every one of my nerve endings.

"Look at me, Rune," he commanded, and I opened my eyes and bit my lip.

"Daxon," I cried, and he pressed his mouth over mine to muffle my screams of pleasure, and then we both fell over the edge.

"Sweetheart," he murmured into my lips, kissing me like he couldn't get enough. He pulsed inside of me, his release hot and heavy as his entire body shook.

We slept just like that for the rest of the night, him still inside of me.

And I didn't think of anything but him...and Wilder, for the whole night.

*S*pending the day on my own after Daxon slipped out of my room in the early hours of the morning felt like torture...which meant that I inevitably thought about Sterling. I should have known that Alistair would send out his men to find me... It was always only going to be a matter of time. I should have been more prepared. As much as my ex was the biggest asshole in the world, he would always be the guy that didn't want others to play with his toys. He would always be determined to get back what he claimed as his...me, in this case.

I decided right then and there that I would rather die than ever go back to that life.

Even though Sterling was gone, I knew there would be more that would come. After all, where one roach appeared, a dozen others lingered in the shadows. Isn't that how the saying went?

The question was, how long did I have before the other roaches appeared?

Alistair might have thought of me as dirt on the bottom of his shoes before, but after what I'd done to him, he'd demand revenge and my suffering. He'd always been vindictive like that. Although, if someone had cut out my eyeball, maybe I'd be a little vindictive too.

Not that the bastard hadn't deserved it.

I wondered how Sterling had found me. I'd been so careful to cover my tracks. I realized that somehow in the last few weeks, I'd become complacent. I'd forgotten that this town was a temporary stop to hide from Alistair and that the plan had been all along to never stop running. Instead, somehow, I let myself make friends, pretend this was my home. And then of course there was the matter of Dax and Wilder, the two alphas who'd entered my life like a tornado—overbearing and unstoppable.

The thought of leaving them felt like a knife wound to the heart.

It was still hard to wrap my mind around the fact that Daxon had dealt with Sterling for me. I...loved him for that. My heart clenched, thinking of his protectiveness. I still couldn't believe that he cared enough to do something at all, let alone...kill the guy.

I stared out the window and wondered, not for the first time, when had I begun to accept that it was normal behavior that the people around me didn't care about me at all? What did that say about me?

The more I thought of Sterling, the more I rocked on my heels and hugged myself, needing to stop freaking out or I'd for sure end up in a full-blown panic attack. What I needed was to remain vigilant, to keep my guard up. Sure,

Daxon got rid of him, but Sterling had probably had time to call Alistair and tell him that he'd found me. Was Alistair going to turn up one day soon with his entire pack?

A shiver raced up my spine, and darkness feathered the edges of mind at the thought of being under Alistair's control once again. Ugly emotions rose through me. Ones of hopelessness, of feeling useless, of being trapped. A sense of heavy, oppressive claustrophobia slid over me.

I sucked in sharp, raspy breaths and shook my arms as they tingled from the fear settling in my veins.

Calm down, Rune. Just breathe.

Easier said than done.

I needed to go for a walk.

I quickly headed out of the inn, enjoying the cool morning breeze as it swished through my hair. I lowered my gaze to the river in front of me. There weren't enough words to describe the beauty of this town, the peacefulness the surroundings offered, so different from where I'd grown up.

I thought that a walk would help me ignore my maddening thoughts. But it seemed they had followed me out here. I turned and decided that I had to do something other than let my mind stew, so I strolled across the green lawn, past the inn and onto the main road. Surprisingly, there were more people about than there had been for a few days. They moved around, going in and out of stores, minding their own business, though the lack of eye contact with each other was obvious. The tension between the packs still lingered, and I shook my head, thinking of how badly everything at the town hall had gone the other night. I also didn't miss the snide glances they were throwing me as I passed by.

Evidently I was still murder suspect number one.

I tried to turn my mind to other things. Like how easily Daxon and I came together, how I couldn't seem to say no to these Alphas. If I was being truthful with myself, I didn't want to push them away, especially after the incident with Sterling. With Daxon and Wilder, I felt safer than I had my entire life.

The toe of my shoe hit something just then, and I suddenly stumbled forward, my arms pinwheeling for balance. Quickly, I caught myself right before my face hit the ground, and I looked back to the uneven sidewalk, heat blazing over my cheeks at my clumsiness. It was even more awkward to be clumsy in a town full of shifters. I'd never seen anyone here be anything but graceful.

Just another reason I should have known something was different about this town.

I glanced back up and noticed someone watched me from across the road.

His short black hair blew messily in the morning breeze, shaved short at the sides. His gaze narrowed as he stared at me, his shoulders seeming to curve forward like he might attack at any moment. Of course, I could have just been imagining that, until he lifted his head and I recognized him at once.

Daniel.

My stomach tightened at the sight of Eve's boyfriend.

The guy she had been sneaking around with, which now that I thought about it, probably had everything to do with the fact they came from different packs. There were a lot more divisions in this town than I first realized.

Suddenly, he was marching across the road and coming right for me with a forceful expression warring across his face.

My legs moved of their own accord, and I retreated until my back hit the brick wall of a building.

Feet from me, he snapped his head up, his eyes red and puffy, the shadows beneath them dark like he hadn't slept in days...which he probably hadn't.

"You fucking bitch, you killed her," he barked, his arms stiff by his side, hands curled into fists. "I don't care what anyone says, I know you took Eve from me."

I was shaking my head, my breath catching in my throat. "Daniel, I wouldn't. I found her that way. I'm so sorry for your loss, but I didn't do this. There was someone else there who took her life."

A deep rumble rolled over his throat, his chest pumping furiously for air. "Fucking convenient isn't it? You must think we're all idiots in this town. The new girl, who rolled in and pretended she had no idea who we were. The new girl who just happened to be a wolf as well. The new girl who acts so fucking innocent and naïve. Were you jealous of Eve? Was that it?" He shouted the words, his body shaking. "You had her blood all over your stupid hands," he continued, a cry in his voice.

It killed me to hear the hatred in his voice, to hear the reasons why he thought I was guilty. I hated the heartbreak in his gaze. I hated his fear.

He stepped forward, and I jammed my back up against the wall, my heart pounding faster.

"Daniel, don't do something you'll regret." With my words, a growl spilled past my mouth. Where the hell did that come from?

"Killer!" he roared, drawing the attention of two older women who strolled down the sidewalk across the road. They looked in our direction, glaring at me, showing zero sympathy. They wanted me to pay for Eve's death too. I saw it in their icy stares.

What was I saying earlier about this place starting to feel like home?

Sweat dripped down my spine as the world seemed to be closing in around me from every angle. I was a murder suspect, Sterling's arrival in town meant Alistair probably had tracked me down, and on top of all that, I had lost a friend.

Exhaustion drained me, and I was tired of constantly feeling like everyone's punching bag. All I wanted was to survive, to fit in somewhere, and instead, I was becoming the target once again.

A ball of emotions wedged itself under my rib cage, making each breath a struggle. I trembled and ached all over as I questioned all my life decisions, even though so much had been out of my control.

Daniel's brow furrowed across the bridge of his nose as he studied me from behind hooded eyes. "You're going to pay." His threat fell from his lips as he lunged at me, his hand coming for my throat.

Panic jolted through me, and instinct had me throwing my arm up to block his assault, then I ducked at the absolute last second. A breath's whisper of air brushed across my back as his fist slammed into the wall, missing me.

He hissed.

I spun to him, my hands fisted. I wasn't a fighter, but the silver glint in his eyes promised me pain. But fuck that, I wasn't going to just sit back and take it. Not anymore.

It was strange that my initial reaction was to be ready for battle and defend myself, something I'd certainly never done with Alistair.

"Daniel, please." My feet slipped backward as he came for me.

A shadow emerged from the store behind Daniel, and suddenly, he was being dragged backward by the scruff of his neck.

"That's enough," Mr. Jones snarled, holding onto the boy who he'd snapped around to face him. Mr. Jones looked so much bigger than Daniel, his white hair wild and barely tamed by his bowler hat, and his huge blue eyes gleaming with frustration. He was an older man, yet he handled himself with ease, yanking the boy about like he weighed nothing. "Do you think it's smart to attack an innocent person because you're angry, boy?"

Daniel shoved away from Mr. Jones' grasp, his face burning red. "Innocent." He laughed bitterly at the word. "That bitch killed Eve," he spat, his eyes tearing up as he pointed at me accusingly. "And she deserves to pay for it."

It seemed we'd managed to gather a small crowd of busybodies stopping to watch the commotion. They all turned their attention to me with hatred in their accusing eyes, lips curled into frowns. I lowered my attention to my shaking hands, wanting to run and hide.

"Did he hurt you, Rune?" Mr. Jones asked, and when I lifted my head, I noticed Daniel was bolting down the sidewalk, making his way toward the bridge over the river. He was gone in an instant, yet I felt like a bug under a microscope with everyone still watching me.

My skin crawled, and I turned without answering, desperate to get the hell out of here, hating how everyone judged me.

"Come into the café, I have some tea I need you to try," he cajoled.

My pulse buzzed, and I paused, twisting my head to look at him. "You don't blame me for Eve's death?" I whispered.

He shook his head at me like I was crazy. "Grief can do horrendous things to people. Now come inside, girl, away from all the busybodies." He stretched an arm out to me, his palm outward in a welcoming gesture.

He was wearing another well-fitted suit with pinstripes that made it easy to imagine we were in a nineteen-twenties movie, and he was welcoming me into his speakeasy or something. Well, maybe his white apron didn't exactly fit the image, but it was quite the presentation...

I didn't wait a second longer, glad for someone to extend me an olive branch. I was desperate at this point. He swept me into his café in a whirl, the aroma of coffee wafting through the air. The smell alone had my muscles easing. Something about coffee had always automatically calmed me.

Stepping deeper into the café as Mr. Jones let go of my hand, I studied the two other customers inside, each sitting at a different table, one reading the paper, another on his phone, while enjoying a cup of Mr. Jones' brew.

"You really should come by more often," Mr. Jones said, interrupting my thoughts, and I glanced over to him as he stepped behind the counter. Like the last time I came in here, it made me feel like I'd stepped back in time with the old-fashioned décor and cash register, plus those huge, metal espresso machines in the background. I found myself lurching to the array of baked cakes and pastries behind a glass cabinet on the counter. I was ready to inhale them all and drown in their sugary goodness to forget all my troubles. A sugar coma sounded nice right about now.

"I definitely need to visit more often." I was a sucker for treats, but hey, everyone had their weakness. Mine just happened to come in the form of pastries. Almond croissants, cinnamon rolls, Danishes, eclairs, tarts. My mouth was salivating, and I glanced up to Mr. Jones, who had his back turned to me, preparing my tea I could only assume.

"Thank you for helping me. It seems everyone else was intent on just watching."

He shifted to the counter between us and set down an oversized ceramic mug painted with stars and the moon. When he looked over to me, his dark framed glasses slid down his nose, and he pushed them back up. "There's been a lot of tension in town lately, and it's easy to turn against each other. Some days, it's difficult to even discern between those who live in this town and our cousins in the wild." He laughed to himself, which amused me.

I smiled at him because as I watched Mr. Jones pouring a green colored tea into the mug from a glass pot, he was the complete opposite of wild wolves. "I would love to try that Nutella pastry, please. It looks delicious."

"I might have been offended if you didn't ask," he teased and hastily plated the treat. "Take a seat, madam, and I'll bring it all out to you."

I moved to take a seat on a small table right by the window where the sunlight made it a perfect spot.

Sitting down on the wooden chair, I stared out toward the mountains in the distance, and the earlier anxiety started to crawl through me the more I thought about the incident with Daniel. He was so adamant that I'd killed Eve, to the point where he attacked me. What would have happened if Mr. Jones hadn't come to help me? Would anyone else come to my aid, or would they cheer for me to be beaten?

I shivered at the thought.

I'd done nothing wrong, and a part of me warned me that if I never stood up for myself, I'd always be walked over. I'd finally made a stand against Alistair and even to Sterling to an extent, so I'd do it again to Daniel and anyone else who blamed me wrongly.

I would find my feet and fight to prove my innocence to everyone in town. That included standing up to Alistair should he show up. Though doubt quickly crept over me at the last thought.

There had to come a point though when even I had enough of always being the weak one.

Mr. Jones arrived at my table and set down the pastry and cup of green tea. "I call it my calming blend. It may not taste the best, but drink it all, and I promise it will help." His smile was infectious, and I nodded, half choked up over him being so nice to me. It was people like him that made me want to call Amarok my home...if they'd have me here of course.

Once Mr. Jones returned to the counter for the new customer who'd walked into the café, I picked up the flaky pastry and bit into it. I moaned at the buttery taste, the sweetness from the Nutella bursting over my taste-buds. I might have just had a small orgasm in my mouth from how incredible it tasted. Before I knew it, I was licking my fingers and glancing over to the glass cabinet for more goodies. I should probably drink the tea first though.

The cup was not as hot as I'd expected when I picked it up, and it carried a scent of berries and grass. I wasn't sure if I should plug my nose and guzzle it, or pour it outside the window. I didn't want to offend the man though, especially since he kept sneaking looks at me to see how I was enjoying my snack, so I took a small sip. Warmth rushed over my tongue, along with a slightly bitter taste, but at the back of my throat, it brought up a beautiful taste of blueberries. I couldn't even explain clearly everything I was tasting, but I kept drinking it, cringing at the initial taste and savoring the aftertaste. In the end, I decided I liked it.

Mr. Jones swept past my table once more, studying me. "What's the verdict? Wasn't too bad, right?"

I shook my head. "Strangely, it's growing on me. I might even have a second cup."

He laughed, throwing his head back. "I can officially say no one has ever asked for a second cup of my calming tea, but I recommend only one a day. How about I bring you another pastry?"

"Yes please." I lounged in my seat as he wandered back to the front of the café, and I couldn't remember the last time I'd felt so relaxed, so calm. Whatever was in that tea, I needed more. Maybe he had tea bags I could take back to my room for when things got out of hand, which seemed like a constant issue in this town...and in my life.

A tingle danced over my fingers, and when I lifted my hands, they seemed to glow. "Wow!" I looked around the café, the whole place now looking like it glittered. Had Mr. Jones switched on some glittery lights? I got to my feet, stretching and feeling more alive than I had in forever. I bathed in how liberated I felt, how all I cared for was how much things sparkled. I wandered across the room to where a man, maybe in his forties, enjoyed a mug of what looked like sparkling coffee.

Immediately intrigued, I slipped into the seat across from him. "I hope you don't mind me joining you?" I asked. "I just couldn't help but wonder what you're drinking? It looks incredible."

He lifted his gaze as he lowered his mug from his lips, my attention following his brew.

"You mean the latte?" His voice held a hint of curiosity.

I nodded and feverishly licked my lips, drawing the man's attention. He might have been older than me, but there was something rugged about him, and the corner of his eye glinted from the sunlight, giving him a sweet look.

"Would you like a taste?" he asked, already handing over his cup.

I nodded eagerly, unsure what was coming over me. Something in the back of my head told me this was weird, but the voice couldn't overpower the lightness in my chest I was feeling suddenly, like I could fly if I wanted to. "I never thought you'd ask. I love sparkly things."

He gave me a weird look as I reached out to grab the cup, our fingers brushing as we made the transfer...which had him straightening in his seat. I didn't waste a moment thinking about that though and sipped the coffee down. Nutty and creamy, but... I blinked down at the beverage. "This doesn't taste special."

"What do you consider special? Would you like me to get you some sugar?" He started to shift in his seat to get up.

I shook my head and set the mug back across the table in front of him, then looked at the man. "You don't seem to hate me," I said as my legs brushed against his under the table, and I couldn't hold back the flirty smile I gave him. Something felt different inside me, almost playful and blurry at the same time.

But just as quickly, he drew back his legs away from me and shifted in his seat uncomfortably. "I know who you are, but there's no reason for me to hate you. I also know that you are with Wilder, and I have no intention of getting on his bad side. If you'll excuse me." The man finished his coffee in two gulps, then climbed to his feet before making a beeline for the exit.

Well, that was rude. I just wanted someone to chat with. When I glanced around, the other man had his nose deeply in the paper, and before I knew it, I was strolling over to him, swinging my hips, feeling especially giggly.

"Rune, honey." Mr. Jones' voice came from behind me suddenly. I spun around and broke into a giggle like I was a little kid who'd just discovered how to twirl.

"Oh, will you spin with me?" I ran my fingers up his arm, discovering he had way more muscles than his suit revealed. "Mr. Jones, you're hiding a hot bod under there, aren't you?"

He half grinned and took my arm in his. "It seems my brew may have made you a bit too relaxed. How about I walk you home?"

Before I could respond, he called out instructions to the waitress who worked with him, and then we were outside.

"I don't know what was in that calming tea, but I'd like to place an order for a pack of one hundred teabags."

He laughed even louder at me then. "Those are not for sale, but something I offer to special customers when they need some time out."

"Maybe you should take me over to Daxon or Wilder's place." I glanced over my shoulder down the sidewalk we strolled along, tugging against Mr. Jones' hold, but his hand swung around my back, drawing me to focus on going forward.

"Oh trust me, Rune. You will sleep the moment your

head hits the pillow, and it will be the best sleep you've had in ages."

I stumbled alongside him, and yet the whole time, I kept feeling like I'd forgotten something important, something that sat on the back of my mind like a mountain.

*T*he entire night had been a blur. I'd slipped in and out of dreams, and my thoughts raced over the events at the town hall. At how quickly everything had spiraled out of control. Though in truth, that was just another normal night if it involved Daxon and me. His presence alone rubbed me the wrong way, and all I wanted was to smash my fist into his face. Fuck, I always seemed so out to control around him, and he gave just as good as I delivered.

He may have a pack who worshipped him and just as many women in town who were desperate for his ass, but something was seriously wrong with the guy. The Alpha image he presented to everyone wasn't the real him, and that part irked me to high hell. Because if he couldn't be himself in his own hometown, then could he be trusted with anything? With anyone?

And that included my girl, Rune. The moment I'd picked up her scent at the town hall the other night, so had Daxon. I'd seen it in the way he stiffened, how he turned to the door to go to her, and well, I lost control. Then shit went sideways from there.

Fucking asshole.

Amarok was a special place, and neither of us were ready to part ways with our home, with our heritage. The location had been passed down from one family to the next in both our pack lines. Centuries ago, two Alphas moved to this land, friends who agreed to build a haven for wolf shifters, a place away from humans. Somewhere for them to run wild in the woods and avoid persecution and being hunted. The place was enormous, much larger when the surrounding woods were taken into account. Plenty of space for two packs to cohabitate. And from what I understood, there had never been a war between the Bitten and Lycan who lived here...well, until now.

This wasn't really just about Rune though. The trouble had started with Arcadia and then just got worse from there.

It just so happened that Rune had upped the stakes. I was not going to lose her to him.

Thinking of the past only had me growling under my breath, and I hated how a single memory could destroy you. I marched across the lawn along the river's edge, needing to get outside, and yet I found myself heading over to the inn to check in on Rune. I hadn't seen her since the town hall incident, having spent the past few days repairing the damage caused. The whole time, Rune consumed my thoughts, her kisses, her soft, curvy body under mine, her moans demanding more. Fuck, I still had her scent in my nostrils, and my cock twitched, succumbing to desire. She reminded me of something deeper and darker in my soul, and I wanted more, so much more than a single moment of pleasure.

I had every intention of claiming her as mine, keeping her by my side.

Mate, my wolf snarled in my chest, like he had been doing each time I thought of her.

She was going to devastate me, I knew this, but I was going into this with my eyes and heart wide open regardless.

My wolf echoed my sentiments with growls, and I strolled quicker. When I lifted my head, my gaze landed on Rune being held up by Mr. Jones as they seemed to almost stumble around to reach the main entrance to the inn. Even from twenty feet away, her soft giggles reached me.

Fire erupted in my chest to see that old man's arm around her arm, and jealousy rose through me. Logic told me he wouldn't make a move, seeing he had his own mate and was about five hundred years older than her. But I'd seen the way other men stared at Rune, like they might sacrifice their own life for a moment with her.

Fuck it.

Before I knew it, I stormed after them, my heart slamming into my rib cage.

But Rune turned her head to me as if sensing my approach before I reached them, and her smile melted my very soul.

"Wilder's here!" she cooed, and she smiled a bit too much, laughed a bit too hard. I loved seeing her less anxious, but something was different about her.

Mr. Jones paused and twisted around to also greet me

with a grin as Rune slipped from his grasp and ran to me. To have said I wasn't ecstatic about her excitement would make me a liar because to have a goddess like her running to me like nothing else mattered, to see the glint of happiness in her eyes, to watch her gorgeous breasts bouncing beneath the blue summer dress she wore, strangled my heart at how much I needed her. The fabric hugged her tiny frame, the buttons running down pulled taut across her chest, and the skirt fell down to her gorgeous thighs loosely. Her short sleeves had slipped down slightly over her shoulders, revealing sun-kissed skin I craved to taste.

To be wanted by such a beauty could undo a man, and as she leapt into my arms, I lost myself. I embraced her, memorizing how she fit against me, her body so soft and all fucking mine.

"I missed you," she whispered with rushed breaths. "Did you miss me too? I haven't been able to stop thinking about the way your tongue licked every inch of me. But if you want me, you'll have to catch me first."

Her words were exquisite and came at me so fast, so unexpected, that it took me a bit to work out where they came from. Plus, if we were anywhere but in open view, I'd have already ripped off her underwear. My hunger for her rose through me, as did my wolf, reminding me she was ours and that we had to fucking mark her already, to stop wasting time or it'd be too late.

"It seems I've already caught you, but flattery will get you everywhere," I whispered, grinning a bit too wide.

Her giggles covered me in goosebumps, the kind that set me on the edge of arousal. Did she have any idea what she did to me? A single word had me captivated, a touch made me mad, her body made me hers to command.

She pressed her mouth to mine, and the world around me vanished. I should have lowered her back to her feet until I got her indoors, but temptation is a wicked thing. I leaned in and sucked her lower lip between my teeth, then inhaled her sweet, honeyed scent.

Fuck, I had to have her again.

Everything about her swallowed me and left my mind fogged.

Mr. Jones cleared his throat. "Well, I will let you two be."

Having completely forgotten about him, I broke from Rune and let my gorgeous girl slide down my body, adoring the sensation of her breasts rubbing against me, trying not to think about how much I desperately wanted to rip her dress off.

Sure, I'd initially thought we should talk about her ex and the way she'd reacted the other night. But no one said we couldn't fuck first.

Rune frowned at me, then slung her arms around my middle, her sullen expression the opposite of how she was seconds earlier.

"What's going on, gorgeous?"

She pursed her lips, and I raised my attention to Mr. Jones. "What happened to her?"

He gave me a sheepish look. "There was a slight altercation outside my café with Daniel trying to attack Rune for Eve's death. So I gave her some of my calming tea as she was worked up."

"What the hell, you made her high with your happy

tea herbs?" My voice rose more than I expected, but that explained everything about the way Rune was acting.

"I'm not high," Rune chirped, just as someone emerged from around the corner of the inn in front of us. Before I lifted my gaze to see who it was, Rune squealed with excitement and suddenly darted from my side.

She threw herself into Daxon's arms as she had done to me earlier, and I hissed under my breath, fire erupting from my chest at her reaction. My hands curled into fists, and while I didn't finish him the other night at the town hall meeting, I might very well just drown the fucker in the river to get him out of my face for good. And most importantly, to drag Rune out of his arms.

"Well then," Mr. Jones murmured, his voice suddenly shuddering. "Look at the time, I do believe the lunch time rush is about to start. I better get back."

He was gone in seconds, and I didn't even care that he lied about the lunch rush. I marched over to Daxon, who held my girl. I wanted to burn the whole fucking town down at the sight.

"For fuck's sake," I spat.

But it was Rune who responded and swung around to stand between us. "No! No one is fighting. Can't you two just get along?" Her voice quivered like she might either lose her voice at any second or pass out.

"What did you do to her?" Daxon snapped, his gaze darkening toward me, one hand gripping Rune's arm to keep her close to him, while I held the other arm, refusing to let her go.

"Do you feel dizzy?" she asked, teetering on her feet. "Why is the sun so bright today?"

"Old man Jones thought it would be nice to calm her down with one of his concoctions after Daniel blamed Rune for Eve's death."

"Fuck me! Why would he give her that? And why did she drink it? It tastes like ass." He shook his head as she practically purred against him. "Daniel is going to regret ever talking to Rune," he said, cracking his neck as a shadow slid over his expression.

"Like fuck you will. Leave him to me," I barked.

"Hey," Rune said, getting us both to look down at her. "If you two are just going to fight, let me go. Screw the both of you." Then she broke into hysterical laughter. "I guess I've already done that with you both already," she said, rather amused at herself.

I huffed, ready to explode, sucking every ragged breath. "You slept with her?" I demanded.

Daxon studied me intently, the curl on the corner of his mouth giving me his answer, and I shredded on the inside, unsure how to feel aside from the fury lashing me. I'd been down this path before with him, promised myself I'd have nothing to do with him, let alone be involved with the same woman.

My head spun, and my hands twitched with an urgency to rip his heart right out of his chest. I snarled out of rage.

"You've lost control of your pack," he hissed through clenched teeth. "If Daniel hurts her, I'll kill him myself."

Fury crackled down my spine. "Is that so?" A thunderous growl ripped my past my throat as I only saw red.

He laughed, the sound cold and venomous. For a second, something flickered in his gaze, something unrecognizable. Like there was a monster lurking inside the Alpha. It was the only way to explain who looked at me behind those deepening eyes.

Suddenly, a slight weight pulled at my hand, and I flicked my gaze to Rune, who'd passed out between us, her head slouched backward, her eyes shut. Us holding her arms were the only reason she hadn't collapsed to the ground.

"Sonofabitch, Daxon, look what you did." I snatched Rune and swept her into my arms. Her soft body curled in against my chest, and I growled that I'd let myself get distracted instead of focusing on her. My heart hammered at seeing the little thing so high on tea leaves, she'd fallen unconscious.

"You think this is my fault?" he snarled.

"Well, you bitch endlessly about everything."

"Fuck you!"

I used my foot to pry open the door and marched into the inn. Jim stood behind the bar, serving a drink, his head jerking up at my entrance. Unlike the last time I marched in there after breaking his door, there was no shock on his face, but rather a resignation that while Rune lived here, I wouldn't keep away.

I ignored the other patrons and headed upstairs, Daxon on my heels, grunting like a damn boar. I paused and twisted my head. "Where the hell do you think you're going?"

"If you think I'm leaving her, you're fucking delusional."

My muscles bunched up across my shoulder blades, and I jerked back around, convinced that if there was ever a day I'd end up murdering Daxon...this might be it.

Rune

I WOKE ABRUPTLY, ripped out of sleep with the words, *Please don't stop*, on my lips. The sad part was that I couldn't remember my dream, but my mind flew back to when I had begged Daxon to spank me. I was definitely not the same person who stumbled into this town, but someone who discovered I loved sex more than I ever imagined, and that included having my ass slapped apparently.

Breathing heavily, it took moments for my eyes to focus and take full stock of the fact that I sat upright in my bed with Wilder and Daxon in my room, staring at me.

I blinked at them, unsure if I was still asleep or some weird time shift thing had happened. These two could barely stand each other, yet neither looked dead or beaten up from being in such close proximity to one another.

"Why are you both in my room?" I pushed the hair off my face, noting my brow felt moist from perspiration. "You know it's creepy to break into someone's room and watch them sleep." Looking down, I checked that I was indeed wearing clothes, since for the life of me, I couldn't remember how I got back to my room or even what day it was. I scratched my head, unsure what happened.

"I'm more curious about your dream," Daxon

murmured, the corners of his eyes wrinkling from his smile. "Tell us more." He grinned mischievously, and when I met his gaze, I recognized the look from when he'd claimed me in this very bed. Heat filled my chest at the thought.

Wilder sighed, giving him a wry look, then returned his attention back to me. "What's the last thing you remember?" he asked, sitting at the end of the bed, a bent leg folded in front of him, while Daxon slouched in the chair he'd placed near my bed, like each was vying to be as close to me as possible.

I might take that as a compliment if I wasn't terrified these two would erupt into a war that might destroy the whole inn...as they had done with the town hall. Though that was a strange night on so many levels.

They stared at me, expectedly... Right, they wanted a response. My brain felt like mush though. I licked my dry lips and looked around for my bottle of water, finally tracking it down on my table across the room.

Daxon got the hint and collected it for me. "Thanks," I croaked out and quickly chased away the dryness in my throat with several mouthfuls. Setting the bottle on the nightstand, I shuffled my legs off the bed, so I sat on the edge.

"Okay, so the last thing I recall was being in the coffee shop with Mr. Jones and eating something filled with Nutella. Oh, and he made me a special green tea that tasted bad." I thought hard about what came next, but all I got were patches of memories. Bright sunlight and the encounter with Daniel beforehand...something I preferred not to think about too much. "So you tell me,

how did I get here, as you must know, otherwise why
would you both be in my room? And please don't tell me
I did something super embarrassing like I fell over and
hit my head." I was rambling at this point, but my head
felt like it was spinning, so I really couldn't be blamed.

Wilder didn't so much as blink. "You drank a hallu-
cinogenic tea to relax you to the point that you can't seem
to remember anything you did." The way he said that
made it sound like I'd done this on purpose.

I stiffened in bed and drew the pillow next to me against
my chest. "He said it was just a calming tea. Fuck. Did I do
something crazy after I drank it?" Maybe I should have asked
Mr. Jones more questions, like how relaxed would I feel? Or
simply not drink random homemade remedies going
forward. Hadn't Miyu warned me of something like that?

Daxon snorted, and that sound alone was enough to
make me panic and fumble with the loose strands of hair
hanging over my shoulder. "You were very forthcoming
with demanding I spank you," he said.

My stomach flip-flopped at his words. Please tell me
he was joking.

Wilder shot to his feet, groaning under his breath.
"No one wants to hear that shit," he blurted.

"You're just jealous," Daxon shot back.

"Well, I guess it depends," I began, interrupting them.
"I mean, if I divulged secrets, then yes I want to know." I
half giggled, hoping that I hadn't just divulged every
embarrassing thing about my past. "And as long as I
didn't hurt anyone, then it couldn't have been that bad."

"You did nothing wrong, sweetheart," Daxon

continued while Wilder moved to stand in front of the window, staring outside, his shoulders pulling up, clear he wasn't happy. "But now we all know where you stand with us."

I swung my attention over to him. "What's that supposed to mean?" Apprehension climbed through me at his words, the back of my mouth tasting sour. I almost choked on the taste of trepidation that he was about to brag about our time together, and well, with Wilder already stewing, we were on our way to another massive fight between them.

Daxon reclined in his seat, studying me deeply like he was fishing for me to say the words first.

I frowned and hopped out of bed, not particularly in the mood to play games, seeing as I'd woken up to find the two males watching me. "If you have something to say, then do it, otherwise maybe you two should both leave my room."

Wilder turned to look our way, his pupils darkening in a way that reminded me he was a dangerous Alpha and might leap at Daxon in a heartbeat. They were like a live wire about to strike at any given moment.

"You're such a prick, Daxon," he snapped. Then he glanced over to me. "We both found you outside the inn after Mr. Jones brought you from the coffee shop. You were very spaced out, then you proceeded to tell both of us, quite gleefully, that you wanted to fuck us again."

"I did?" I licked my lips again as nerves danced up my spine, an unsettling feeling twisting in my stomach. I half expected them to jump into a rant, except they both stared at me like somehow they'd been waiting for me to wake up to talk to me about this exact thing.

Despite my heartbeat thumping in my ears, I reminded myself that I was no longer going to be the person who let others push me around and would try to stand up for myself. I stood between them and threw my arms up in frustration.

"What do you want me to say? I'm not sorry for it." I splayed my hands out across my stomach, holding them still to conceal their quiver. "I have nothing to hide, and I'm nothing like your ex, if that's what you're both worried about. Maybe it's better this is out in the open now so we can all talk and be civil."

The looks on both their faces were the opposite of civil, and now my heartbeat echoed in my ears. Instead, they glared at each other.

"Tell me more about your encounter with Daniel?" Wilder asked, breaking the stalemate between the two of them, and his question told me two things. One, he had no plans on leaving my room. And two, Daxon would keep his stubborn ass here too because they were nowhere near finished with me finding myself attracted to them both.

"Mr. Jones told you, I guess?"

Daxon nodded. "Did Daniel hurt you?"

I shook my head. "Mr. Jones stopped him before he got the chance."

The shock on his face was almost humorous. "Appears the old man has some tricks up his sleeves after all."

Daxon said nothing but reclined farther in his chair,

his legs wide, his hands tucked into the pockets of his pants, studying me with a strange look in his eyes, completely ignoring Wilder. Daxon made me feel like a deer spotted in the woods by a wolf. He sat back, unfazed by Wilder, even if they seemed to be mortal enemies, like nothing in the world scared him. Was it strange that I found that both ridiculously alluring and scary at the same time?

"It's good Mr. Jones protected you," Daxon finally answered. "He is good for something at least, but maybe you shouldn't be alone when going out?"

My muscles went stiff, and flames blazed across my mind instantly. "No," I answered. "I am not a helpless woman, and I did a decent job of standing up to Daniel too. I won't become a prisoner in my bedroom." The unspoken words of how they'd already made me a prisoner in the town stretched between us.

Both men watched me with curiosity.

"I don't want you hurt," Daxon told me, his chin jerking upward, while Wilder watched without a word. He stood still as a soldier, expressionless, and I struggled to make sense of either man. They were broody, and their presence alone twisted my gut, sending my emotions and arousal all over the place. Part of me wondered if they finally clashed and destroyed one another, would that be easier for me to just find peace in this town without drama? Or would it in turn ruin me?

"Maybe it's not a bad idea," Wilder said, finally breaking his silence, holding my gaze. Apparently, having them both close to me at the same time did nothing to cool me down, especially when they said shit that got me riled up.

He spoke like he gave me an order, and I narrowed my gaze at him. "Maybe instead of trying to wrap me in bubble wrap, we should work on convincing the town that I'm not the killer."

A loud, abrupt knock came from the door, and I flinched in my skin, shifting toward the entrance.

Daxon shoved to his feet, and Wilder was at my side in a flash, a deep guttural growl in his throat.

"Who is it?" I asked out loud, but Daxon had already crossed the room and thrown open the door. He blocked the doorway, making it impossible for me to see who stood there, but from the hurried whispers and deep tone, it sounded urgent.

Wilder's arm wrapped around my waist, drawing me against him as if he heard something I hadn't.

"Okay, thanks," Daxon stated and turned to face us. "Great news. Someone has just been killed in the exact same way Eve had."

It was hard to think as I made sense of his words, not fully understanding how someone's death was in any way related to good news. I understood instantly his intended response had everything to do with implying if it was a recent kill, it would finally show the whole town it couldn't have been me who killed Eve. Except another innocent person had just lost their life, which begged the question, what the fuck was hunting the locals in town?

"Where? Do we know who it is?" Wilder asked.

"Near the woods behind the town hall. I'm going

there now." Daxon answered, already marching out of the room.

Wilder looked down at me. "Stay here, and I'll swing by later."

"You are out of your mind if you think I'm staying here, waiting." I rushed across the room and stepped into my boots before grabbing my wallet and room key. "I'm coming too."

He shrugged, shaking his head, but he did nothing to stop me. I had to know right away if the murder scene was the same, anxiety swimming inside me. Was it terrible that like Daxon, I suddenly hoped they had been killed in the same manner to prove my innocence?

The weather outside had turned bitter, the wind carrying an icy bite, and bruised clouds stained the sky.

We walked through town, and when we finally arrived at the town hall, I noticed a small gathering of people at the rear of the building. My stomach clenched as I pictured Eve, her throat torn out, her dead eyes holding the terror of what she'd gone through.

I stayed close to Wilder's side, the crowd parting for his arrival. On the other side of the crowd was a tall, proud patch of evergreens that jutted out of the forest.

My gaze instantly fell to the body several feet away, my heartbeat drumming in my chest. Dread clutched my heart, and breathing came too hard as I frantically scanned the face to see if I recognized it.

"You don't have to see this," Wilder whispered in my ear, his hand on my lower back, his warmth doing little to chase away the chill that had settled over my bones.

I stumbled forward, not finding my words, but needing to know if it was the same killer.

Daxon crouched near the victim, his head low, and a low rumble rolling from him telling me that victim had to belong to his pack. It was a young man I didn't recognize. He had short golden hair, a short beard, and casual clothing. Blood pooled around his throat, the flesh torn open, and I hated that I couldn't look away from the gore, from the way I could see bone from where it appeared the head was pulled back for easier access. Something sharp like fangs or claws had been slashed across the flesh, stealing the man's life.

Just as it had Eve's. The killing was too similar to not be the same killer. Both murdered the same way, both not too far from the woods. And by the position of the body, legs pointed toward the trees, one shoe abandoned several feet behind us, I could only assume he was killed in the open and then dragged toward the woods.

But why? To make it look like it was a wild animal and this man had gotten too close to the woods? Did that mean whoever did this lived in this town? I held myself tight, the murder devastating, and with it came the terror that something truly terrifying was watching us.

Wilder stood across from Daxon and crouched down, talking to him with sincerity about the loss.

The more I stared down at this poor guy, the more paranoia flooded me that it might be anyone in town. I glanced around me at the others studying us, dread blanching their expressions. Glancing back, I squeezed my eyes shut and tried to breathe in deep, to focus just on the scent with the hope that maybe I'd smell anything familiar from Eve's murder scene.

With my wolf still blocked inside me, the only smells I got were that of pungent blood, making me sick the longer I smelled it.

I stepped closer to Wilder, who'd stood up from the body. "The kill looks fresh. He's still bleeding as the blood hasn't coagulated yet."

He nodded, his expression strained.

Daxon was on his feet, darkness dancing across his face. "Get her out of here," he barked at Wilder, then he stormed back toward the crowd behind us, yelling orders. Demanding answers.

The anger in his voice was palpable. Daxon wasn't someone who openly seemed to show his emotions, but right now, he was furious.

"Let me take you back home," Wilder insisted, and I didn't protest but turned away from the crime scene, my stomach churning from the sight. Stopping the tears from appearing for his loss, for Eve's, was a losing battle, and I quickly wiped my eyes. I hated how I always seemed to feel too much. Even for practical strangers.

Wilder collected my hand in his, our fingers interlaced, and we made our way back toward the main road.

"Daxon seemed really upset about the victim. Who was he?" I finally asked when we were out of earshot from Daxon.

"Asher Turner. Asher lost his parents at eight to wolf hunters deep in the woods, and Daxon had always had a soft spot for the kid who'd lost everything. He helped find him a family to live with and get homeschooling, and even more recently, he helped him get a job in construction. So this is a huge blow to him."

"That's horrible." I chewed on the inside of my cheek, my heart aching for Daxon. I didn't know if I could ever be the same again after witnessing these senseless murders. I'd seen enough devastation caused by Alistair, but Amarok was a haven for packs and families. It was meant to be safe...or maybe that was just the image I'd painted for myself.

The images of death and so much blood haunted my thoughts, and I pushed down vomit. "It's the same killer," I said.

"I believe so too." His gorgeous green eyes were unfocused as he glanced away, and his hand around mine tightened. "You have to be extra careful around town. I'd die if I found you fucked up like that." He paused at the edge of the road and brought me around to face him, his hands holding my arms. "Promise me you won't go out alone at night, or go anywhere near the woods."

My teeth chattered at the way the fear in his eyes showed through. If a powerful alpha was this scared, then I had everything to worry about.

"How will you find the killer?"

"I'll set up watchers around town and in the woods and start tracking everyone."

"I know shifters have amazing senses. I couldn't smell anything but the blood on Asher, but did you pick up the killer's scent?"

He frowned as his gaze flicked to the town hall grounds behind me. "That's the thing. I should have, except there's nothing there, like it never happened or they made sure to be extra careful to not leave anything of themselves behind."

I blinked at him and looked back over my shoulder to where Asher lay, a shiver covering me at the feeling of being watched. My gaze darted around, but nothing seemed out of the ordinary. Everyone's attention was still focused on the body.

"Let's get going." Wilder drew me away from the town hall. We were halfway up the main road when a rumble from in front of us jerked my head up.

Several feet away, Arcadia strolled toward us, her pitch-black hair perfectly styled to fall over her shoulder, her makeup flawless as usual. In her painted on skinny jeans and her crop top the color of the sun, she looked perfect. As stupid as it sounded, jealousy grew within me to see her looking so beautiful that she could easily be mistaken for a runway model, while I still wore the clothes I'd fallen asleep in after getting high on tea.

We were nothing alike, but then again, Wilder was holding my hand, not hers. Something she noticed instantly, and when her gaze lifted to me, her nose scrunched up with disdain.

"You have really lowered your standards, Wilder." She practically spat the words at him. "Associating with the town killer. Is this your new kink? How long before you tire of fucking this skank?" She stood before us, her shoulders squared, her lips thinned...hatred beaming out of her gaze like spotlights.

"Fuck off, Arcadia, and get out of our way," Wilder snarled, drawing me closer to him, his hand wrapping around my waist protectively.

"Everyone knows you did it, bitch," she snapped at me. "And sooner or later, they'll get tired of you and then you'll be gone, or even better...dead."

Hatred flared across my chest, and I tried to push it down. One thing about Arcadia, you could tell she got off on trying to torment me. Unfortunately for her, I was an expert in dealing with bullies. Alistair had made sure of that. I met her gaze dead on and asked, "I'm curious, how do you comb your hair so your horns don't show?"

Wilder huffed a laugh, while Arcadia seethed, her face reddening. He drew us forward, having no intention of getting out of Arcadia's way. "Let's get a few things straight." The corner of his mouth quirked up. "There is no way Rune killed anyone. For one thing, she was in her room with Daxon and me for most of the day, which was the time Asher was butchered. So how about you really fuck off now and show some respect for his death instead of spreading false accusations. And secondly, if I ever hear you threaten Rune again, you're going to be the one gone..." He left the last part unspoken, but the message was clear. Holy fuck.

Arcadia's mouth dropped open, and she seemed to almost curl in on herself as if ready for the world to swallow her away.

I couldn't deny the satisfaction in seeing her put in her place. After every encounter I'd had with her, to see her practically pissing her pants at Wilder's warning had me smiling like a mad person. We brushed right past her, leaving her a shaking mess behind us.

"Oh shit, that was amazing. Did you see her shock?" I

glanced over my shoulder to where she hurried down the street with her head bowed low.

"She deserves a lot worse," he said. "And like I said earlier, I won't let anything or anyone ever hurt you again."

Butterflies erupted in my stomach. That sounded so fucking good.

"*R*une!" Miyu's voice echoed down the sidewalk as she leaned out of the salon doorway. I'd needed fresh air after spending the previous day stuck in my room at Wilder's command. And one day was enough. So most of the morning, I'd been on the hunt for a coffee shop other than Mr. Jones' place, since I was still embarrassed as could be about what his little calming tea had done to me the other day.

I hadn't been successful.

"Rune," Miyu yelled again, until everyone who was on the street was looking at her waving her hands around in some sort of weird dance like a crazy person.

"I heard you the first time," I snarked when I got a bit closer.

"I know," she said with a wink. "I just felt like embarrassing you."

"Mission accomplished."

She snorted and then opened the door. I didn't work

today, so I definitely had time for some girl time if she wanted it.

I'd kind of been...avoiding her. After that whole town hall disaster when everyone had lost their motherfreaking minds, I wasn't sure what she was thinking about me.

I tried to read her as she led me to a new table set up by the back wall. She seemed perfectly normal though, or as normal as a person like Miyu could be.

"Sit down, sit down!" she ordered as she settled into a seat across the table from me. I belatedly realized what the table was for.

"A nail station?" I asked.

"Yes. Yes. Yes," she said loudly while doing another little weird dance in her chair.

I laughed in delight as I examined all the tools she had set up. There was a bookshelf behind her loaded with what looked like every color of dip and gel polish that the world could possibly contain.

"Do you know how to do nails?" I asked after a moment, and she nodded before pulling my right hand towards her and began to look over my nails critically.

"Yes I do, and we're going to do your ugly ass nails right now while you tell me why you've been avoiding me," she ordered.

Busted. I tried to open my mouth to lie and deny it, and she gave me a long glare before I could say anything, like she could see right through me.

I promptly closed my mouth without a word.

Silence descended, and although Miyu didn't seem to

be feeling the awkwardness at all, I was definitely resisting the urge not to squirm around in my seat.

Miyu hummed as she swiveled her chair around to grab a bowl, filling it with some kind of pink colored liquid before setting it down on the table and forcing all of my fingers into it. She finally turned her attention towards me and just stared at me as if daring me to speak.

I folded immediately like a chump.

"I just didn't know how you've been feeling about everything. If you felt the way everyone else in this town seems to feel at the moment."

"You mean you didn't know if I thought you were a serial killer?" she asked with an impish smile.

The words sounded ludicrous coming out of her mouth, but then Daxon's face sprang into my mind. You never knew who around you was a killer. I'd certainly never thought he could be one.

"Hey, I was just joking," she said softly as she patted my arm.

"Oh, yeah. Sorry, I just got caught in my thoughts for a moment," I told her, pushing everything I'd been thinking about Daxon far, far away for the time being.

She frowned sympathetically as she gently took one of my hands out of the bowl and began to work feverishly on it, her hands flying around so fast, it was hard to keep up with them.

"You know it's so stupid how people are acting," she growled out fiercely. "If I hear anyone say one more thing, I swear I'll gut them, and I've lived around these people for years!" She held up a finger as if she were announcing her vow to a crowd of people, when really, we were all alone in here. I was touched by her loyalty to a girl she didn't know very well.

"I was at the town hall, I know exactly what they're saying," I said with a sigh.

Miyu's face scrunched up like she was thinking hard. "You know, it's weird. I remember walking to the town hall with Rae. I remember sitting down and the meeting starting and everyone discussing Eve. And then I remember people starting to blame you. I intended to stand up and call out their bullshit. But I'm not sure why I didn't... It was all a kind of blur from there. I have this faint recollection of everyone going crazy around me. I mean honestly, I went a little crazy too. I'm pretty sure I pulled Aleshia's hair out and stuffed it down her boyfriend's throat..." she rambled. I laughed, and she grinned at me. "But the details are fuzzy. Like I was there, but I wasn't. Does that make sense?"

I nodded. "It was a strange night. It was like everyone went mad."

"Sometimes, wolves get frisky and riled up before a full moon and during...but it wasn't a full moon and it's never like that," Miyu mused as she filed away at my pinky finger. Hopefully, I would have a nail left after she was done. I wasn't quite sure if she was actually paying attention.

Something rolled around in my stomach as I thought about all the ways people had acted since I'd come here. Like that scene in the grocery store...with Arcadia.

I suddenly really wanted to tell Miyu. I'd never had a girlfriend before. At least not since I was a little girl. And I'd certainly never had a best friend in any sort of meaningful way where someone was your ride or die. I examined her face as she hummed what I was pretty sure was an off-key version of "I'm a Slave 4 U" under her breath.

"Sometimes, it feels like I can affect people's emotions," I blurted out before I could think on it anymore. It had been a thought that had been stirring in my mind for weeks now. Something I hadn't wanted to think about. I really was an expert at avoiding things.

"Like how do you mean?" Miyu said, and in that second, I really loved this girl because there was no judgment in her voice. She wasn't even looking at me like I was crazy. She was just looking at me like I was...interesting.

"Since coming here, there've been a few times where people have just begun acting completely different for no reason." I proceeded to tell her about the grocery store scene with Arcadia and the town hall and the parents at their daughter's grave.

Miyu chewed on her lip, deep in thought after I finished. I waited there for a long minute, sure she was going to throw me out or call the loony bin on me. Finally, she gave me a huge, exuberant smile and gasped, "What if you're like some kind of superhero or something?"

"What? No. I'm not a superhero," I said with a laugh as I settled back into my seat, and she began to work on my nails again. "I'm probably as far away from a superhero as can be. I would run away from my shadow if it wasn't attached to me."

Miyu shook her head as she began to cut away excess

parts of my cuticle. "I don't think you see yourself very clearly, Rune. Or the way others see you."

She shifted in her chair, suddenly nervous about something. "Obviously, you haven't told me very many details about your ex or your old life, but I saw the bruises on your neck that day. I heard the pain in your voice. The courage it took for you to get away from him, to come here, you need to recognize that. You need to use that to help build yourself up. Because you should think of yourself as a hero, Rune. Any time a woman decides she's had enough and she vows to get a better life...she becomes a hero."

A silent tear made its way down my cheek. "I stayed with him forever because he was my true mate. He did awful things, and I never did anything about it. Not until someone basically paved the way for me to get out of there."

"You met your true mate," she gasped, her own eyes glistening with unshed tears. I looked away from her and closed my eyes, remembering for the one billionth time what it had felt like for him to reject me. I let the pain roll over me, over and over again, looking for any signs that I'd healed at all.

And to my surprise, I had. The pain was still there. It would probably always be there, an open wound to remind me the moon goddess had forsaken me. But while the pain used to be like a hot knife slicing and carving its way through my skin until I thought I would die, it now felt like a dull punch. Noticeable but not life-destroying.

"My true mate rejected me," I told her.

She stared at me for a long moment, heartbreak in her eyes. "See, total badass," she finally whispered.

I opened my mouth to immediately object, because that was what I did—I resisted any attempts people made to compliment me or pull me from my self-pity.

Then I stopped. And I actually thought about what she'd said and the wonder in her voice.

I'd heard of some people almost dying when they'd been rejected. It was the story whispered around the campfire, the nightmare single shifters tried not to think about as they waited to find their mate. It was considered the worst thing that could ever happen to you. An act so hideous, that you would exist as half a person for the rest of your life.

Yet here I sat.

I had issues, plenty of them. But after being an abused doormat for years, I had pulled on my boot straps and my metaphorical lady balls, and I'd escaped. I'd even carved my mate's eyeball out to access his safe. And even though I was basically trapped in this town, I was still surviving. I had somehow survived several terrifying encounters with a mysterious beast, I'd found a job, I'd made at least one friend, and I'd opened myself up to the most mind-blowing sex I'd ever had with the two most gorgeous men I'd ever seen.

I wasn't thriving, but I definitely wasn't sucking at life.

Maybe...I actually was a badass.

The thought was life-changing for me. It was like years of self-torment and self-disgust were lifted from my shoulders in that moment. A giggle escaped from my mouth, and soon, Miyu and I were both laughing, although I wasn't sure she actually knew why we were laughing.

"I'm kind of a badass," I shouted with glee, springing from my seat and dancing around the room.

Miyu jumped out of her chair as well, pressed a button on the wall, and music suddenly started. Taylor Swift's "Shake It Off" blasted from speakers in the wall.

We danced and laughed, and I allowed myself to dream about a life that didn't include Alistair or any thoughts of him. I allowed myself to dream of a life where I laughed and danced with abandon, where I lived life without fear of the past or the future. I allowed myself just to be.

It was one of the best moments in my life. And the happiness sparking inside of me...I welcomed it like an old friend that I hadn't seen for a very long time.

And it welcomed me right back.

WE DANCED for nearly an hour and then finally settled back into our chairs, where Miyu went back to work on my nails. I felt closer to Miyu after my revelation, like me letting go of my self-hatred had made room for me to actually be the kind of friend that I wanted to be.

"I slept with both Wilder and Daxon this week," was the next thing I decided to blurt out.

Her eyes widened. "Girl, you are goals," she said, beaming as she knocked the pink polish away and grabbed a bottle of deep red. "I'm painting your nails red because you are the freaking goddess of sex. Now tell me everything."

So I did...with the exception of my suspicions about Daxon. If I could really call them suspicions at this point. I also left out the emotions that had been exchanged and the whole mate thing with Wilder. That felt a little...too private.

Basically, I stuck with dick sizes and sexual prowess in my story.

"Who was the best in bed?" she asked with a grin after I was done.

I shrugged, unable to answer. They'd both been equally mind-blowing in different ways.

"Lucky bitch," she exhaled as she painted another nail.

"So how are you and Rae?" I asked, feeling bad that we'd done nothing but talk about me this whole time. Miyu just had this air about her that made you want to curl up and tell her all your secrets. It was the perfect gift for someone who owned a salon. All her clients basically got to engage in a therapy session every time they came in.

"Ugh, I guess he wants to marry me or something," she said like she was annoyed.

I raised an eyebrow. "And that's a bad thing why?" I asked. She and Rae were basically the cutest thing ever. He seemed to love every ridiculous and wonderful part of her, which sounded pretty great if you weren't super damaged inside about relationships like I was.

Vulnerability shone in her gaze for a moment, and she looked away.

"Hey," I said softly, leaning in since I couldn't reach out and touch her while she was still working on my nails. "What is it? Are things not good?"

She smiled sadly. "Things are wonderful. He treats me like a freaking queen. And he loves me. He really loves me."

"But...?" I pressed.

"But he's not my fated mate. And what if his fated mate, or my fated mate, suddenly appears years from now, after we've been happily married for years. What if we have kids and that happens?" She bit her quivering lip to stop from crying. "We would be ruined. I just... My dad was married before he met my mom," she blurted out. "He was out grocery shopping, getting something his wife needed for dinner, and he saw my mom. She was his true mate. He and my mom tried to resist the bond. But no matter what my dad told himself, he couldn't ever feel the same way about his wife after that. And she couldn't stand to know that every time he was with her, he was longing for my mother. It destroyed her. And my dad still feels the guilt even twenty-something years later!" Miyu let out a shivering gasp. "What if that happens to me?"

Her dad's story was one of the saddest things I'd ever heard. As a shifter, you weren't even guaranteed that you would meet your fated mate. So for her dad to have met his...after marrying someone else, that was pretty devastating.

I hesitated before I said anything, unsure of what to say. A love expert, I was not. Suddenly, an overwhelming feeling of peace passed over me. For just a second, I just knew with perfect certainty that everything with Miyu would be all right.

"Wow, babe. Are you all right?" she said anxiously, yanking on my arm.

My eyes flickered open, and I shook my head, feeling like I'd just been underwater or something.

"You just went scary still and your eyes rolled to the back of your head," Miyu went on, continuing to pull on my arm like she was afraid I was going to disappear.

"Yeah, that was kind of weird," I murmured, firmly pushing whatever had just happened into my 'save for another date' pile that was rapidly growing.

"Miyu, I may be the last being who should be commenting on love or fated mates or anything like that at all actually. But I can tell you I know from experience that your fated mate isn't always your be-all and end-all. They aren't guaranteed to be the most amazing person you've ever met. So if you think you have met your person in Rae, I don't think you should let that go. If you feel right about Rae, you shouldn't let fear get in the way. I think it's all going to work for you, Miyu. I don't know why I think that, but I really do."

She looked at me hopefully, and once again, I was floored with how much this girl seemed to value me as a person and what I thought. I just hoped I'd given her the right advice.

"Thank you," she breathed.

"No, thank you," I whispered back. We didn't talk for a few minutes as she finished putting polish on my nails, each lost in our thoughts.

"Ugh, what other deep conversation can we have?"

Miyu finally said with a watery chuckle after she'd finished my last nail.

I had to admit, they looked great.

Daxon's face filled my head just then. Since we were all about discovery today, might as well find out more about him.

Miyu got up and grabbed us both some Diet Cokes from a fridge in the back room and then came back with cups loaded with pebble ice. I freaking loved this woman.

"So what was Daxon like when he was young?" I asked as we both sipped our drinks. All I needed now was a Swig cookie. I'd happened upon one of those places during my road trip and that place was the bomb.

Miyu crinkled her nose as she thought about my question. "Daxon's always been larger than life. The popular kid. Always the golden boy."

I snorted when she said that, thinking of my nickname for him. It probably wasn't very original.

"But..." She trailed off.

"What?" I asked, taking a long sip from my straw.

"It always seemed kind of fake to me, ya know?" she finally said.

I cocked my head, surprised that she had seen anything amiss. He'd certainly fooled me.

"He was just always on, ya know? Besides the whole mess with Arcadia...and I guess his thing with Wilder lately..."

I flinched at the reminder of his ex.

"He has just always seemed too perfect to me. And especially with some of the rumors about what people heard at night—"

"What do you mean?" I asked, my craving for a cookie now forgotten.

She gave me an apologetic look. "People would hear screams coming from their house. Like someone was being tortured...like Daxon was being tortured."

My gaze widened, and my heart ached for him. Something told me Miyu probably wasn't that far off the mark, judging by the darkness I saw hiding in Daxon's gaze.

"But he always seemed so freaking put together at school, it just never felt like any of that was real. I heard sometimes the police were called by the people that heard the screams, but they never saw anything amiss. And I mean really...was anyone going to go up against the alpha and really accuse him of anything? It was practically suicidal that some people called the police in the first place since the police work for the alphas."

Cold fury rushed through me at the thought of Daxon's father hurting his son. "What happened to Daxon's father? And I guess Wilder's for that matter?"

Miyu pursed her lips. "It all was kind of strange. I mean, I was pretty young when it all happened. But I know Wilder challenged his father and won. And Daxon's father just disappeared. They found his body in the woods, ravaged by bears or something, I guess. And that was that."

My mouth dropped in shock at what she'd just said. But before I could ask anything else, since I had about a million questions, Rae walked through the front door.

Miyu immediately jumped from her seat and launched herself at a surprised and honestly relieved looking Rae. "Baby," she squealed, peppering his face with kisses.

I had a feeling I was probably going to be attending a wedding in the near future. I decided it was probably best to give the happy couple some time to themselves, since Miyu looked like she was about to start stripping.

"How much do I owe you?" I called out.

Miyu continued to kiss Rae's face and waved a hand at me distractedly. "On the house, babe. It was good practice for me," she said between kisses.

I shook my head and slipped some money next to her drink before sliding past them to get to the front door.

Neither of them even noticed I'd left. Yep, I was thinking Miyu and Rae were going to be just fine.

"Please!!!!!!" The dead man's cries rang through the air, the perfect soundtrack if you asked me. This was the third enforcer in the last month that Rune's ex had sent. It was the busiest my little cabin had ever been. I was kind of hoping her ex's pack had a limitless number of people to send. A guy could get used to this. If I wasn't careful, I was going to get addicted and end up spending all my time down here.

I smiled to myself. Nah, that wouldn't happen. There was nothing in existence I could be addicted to more than Rune. At this point, she wasn't just an obsession, she was something I needed in order to keep breathing. If she ever got away from me...

Whoops. I couldn't think about that.

I'd accidentally stabbed my babbling prisoner in his femoral artery at the thought of Rune leaving, and blood had begun to gush everywhere.

Well dang it. I'd been trying to work on my knife carving skills with this one, see just how thin I could make the cuts as I peeled the guy's skin off. He'd kept trying to wolf out on me, but as soon as I would make a slice, his magic would putter out, and he'd return to human form.

I guessed this was going to be over quick. I sighed and wrapped a tight bandage around the wound to try and stop some of the bleeding, but I'd stabbed way too deep. I mean, the guy's leg was close to coming off.

I'm sure there would be more where this one came from.

I sighed as I slit the guy's throat, pissed that I hadn't made his pain last longer. I at least should have made it as painful as what he and his alpha had in store for my girl.

My betas had caught this one lurking right outside the town border, a veritable trove of pictures of Rune in his car. Evidently, a lot of the members of Rune's pack had a hard-on for her. This one especially. I doubted Rune would have made it back to him. His alpha really should be smarter when choosing people to send.

Better yet, he should come himself.

Just the thought had me salivating. I'd been planning Alistair's death for weeks. Rune had let his name slip, and I'd been obsessed with learning as much as I could about my competition as possible. And he *was* competition. No matter what he did to her, as long as he was alive, I would be competing with him for her heart. Rune could hate him more than anything, and it still wouldn't completely sever the ties that the moon goddess, in her stupidity, had created.

That's what made being rejected by your mate that

much worse. Because even when you should have been rid of them, there was always a part of them with you, no matter what you did.

Which was why Alistair was a dead man. I would just bide my time. Rejected or not, I knew for a fact he was obsessed with Rune. And he was never going to have the chance to get her back again.

It was bad enough that Wilder was sniffing at her... and sleeping with her any chance he could get. I would have killed him off if I hadn't known how much she liked the asshole. I could feel my mating bond somehow forming any time I was around her though. I wasn't sure how that was happening, but I wasn't about to push back on it.

Rune Celeste Esmeray was the most perfect creation I'd ever stumbled across. And I was never going to lose her.

I forced myself to concentrate on the clean-up I had ahead of me. Rune never strayed far from my thoughts though. She'd become the focal point of my world.

After cutting the guy into pieces and placing him on the tarp I'd use to drag him to my very well-fed pigs, I began to head up the stairs. Thank goodness for my shifter strength, since this guy had been a heavy motherfucker.

I'd just reached the top of the stairs when I heard a knock on the front door.

I rolled my eyes. This place and my pasttimes were a secret. But there was one person who I'd made the mistake of trusting my secret with...a long, long time ago.

And I'd regretted that as soon as the words had left my mouth.

I didn't bother cleaning the blood off of me. If she was coming here, it meant that she needed a reminder of just what I was capable of.

I swung the door open, and there she was, the bitch of my existence.

"Arcadia, what a surprise. I would say it's a good one, but you know I don't like liars."

Arcadia's face fell. I stared at my ex. I'd used to think she was the kind of beauty men fought wars over. She'd come into my life at my darkest moment, and I'd worshipped at her feet like she was an angel sent to save me.

I'd never been more wrong about anything in my entire life.

Now that I could compare her to the perfection of Rune, I wanted to punch myself, somehow travel back in time and tell that guy to wait. That being lonely and miserable would be worth it, because someday, Rune would come into town.

I tried not to have regrets in my life. I tried to think of everything as a learning moment.

Arcadia was a lesson I'd give almost anything not to have learned.

She was dressed to kill, so little clothing on that she might as well have been wearing nothing.

Her eyes were devouring me, the blood covering me doing nothing to lessen her appetite.

"I thought we could talk," she purred, reaching out to touch me before thinking twice.

"You thought wrong," I told her, beginning to turn away. Arcadia panicked, and this time, she reached out to grab my arm, the blood on me making her fingers slip against mine.

"Daxon, please. What will it take for you to forgive me?" she asked brokenly.

I sighed, thinking of the date with Rune I needed to get ready for and the body I still needed to feed to the pigs. Not to mention the rest of the mess still waiting for me in that room.

"There's no forgiveness necessary," I said coldly. "I don't care enough about you to need to forgive you for anything."

The words sliced through her, and she withdrew her hand like she'd been burned. She rubbed at her chest, her lips quivering and tears threatening in her gaze as she looked at me like I'd broken her heart.

When was she going to realize that I knew it was impossible for that to happen because she didn't have a heart to begin with.

As I watched her try to put on her usual show, I began to wonder how easy it would be to get away with her death. My gaze bored into her as I thought about how I would do it. I'd have to be especially cruel, the bitch would probably get off on my usual tactics just because she was actually getting attention from me.

"You're my true mate," Arcadia pleaded.

Hmm. That was a new one.

I snorted, then couldn't hold the rest of my laugh in. It rolled out of me until I was having to wipe a tear from my eye. The girl could probably have a career as a comedian.

When I finally opened my eyes and was able to stop laughing, the tearful act Arcadia had been going for had been changed to rage. That was what I'd been waiting for.

"I know you felt it—the bond as it formed. I was there for you when no one else was. That alone should show you I was your true mate. You have to remember. I know you remember!" she seethed.

I snapped and suddenly pulled my favorite knife from the back of my pants and held it against her neck, a small drop of blood dripping down her throat as I cut into the skin.

Arcadia's eyes sparked, and not with fear, like somehow, she'd just convinced me to engage in some deadly sex game or something.

The only sex games I was interested in playing were with Rune, thank you very much. And there would be nothing deadly involved because if that girl ever died, I'd be following her quickly into the great beyond. My fate had somehow become forever entwined with hers.

"Let me tell you something, you little bitch. What I remember is you taking advantage of me when I didn't have anyone else. I remember you drawing me in with that cesspool between your legs. I remember you playing me and pretending to be someone you weren't. And then I remember you pretending to be pregnant, knowing children would mean everything to me, all while screwing Wilder." I grinned evilly, and for the first time, I let my inner demons show on my face.

Arcadia's skin paled, and the scent of her fear grew thick and heady around me. "You're alive because I allow you to live, never forget that. There will be a day when I decide your life is over," I told her silkily. "Remember that before you ever come here again."

She pissed herself and began to tremble against me, and I shook my head in disgust at her weakness. Without warning, I pulled my knife away from her and pushed her away. She fell to the ground and began to crawl towards her car, sniveling and moaning as she scrambled to get away from me.

The sight was extremely...satisfying. And also another huge reminder of what an idiot I'd been as a pup. I shook my head and turned back to go and clean up my mess, confident that Arcadia would never dare to come here again.

And if she did, well I guessed she was just asking for me to kill her, wasn't she?

With that delightful thought, I pushed Arcadia out of my head and replaced her with the goddess I'd be seeing in just a bit.

Time to get to work. I had a date to get ready for.

"*R*une, I can't believe you've never been to a carnival," said Rae as we approached the fair.

"Babe," Miyu hissed under her breath as she jabbed him in the ribs. "Geez, is your sensitivity radar on the brink tonight?" She eyed him, then me with an apologetic frown, and I laughed.

"It's not a big deal," I said. "I mean, I've seen them on television and have the general gist of them."

"If it makes you feel any better," Daxon interrupted after not saying much for the walk across the bridge and the open land to where the carnival was set up, "this is the first time I've attended one in the past ten years."

Miyu's mouth dropped open in a shocked expression. "Carnival Utopia has come to our town every year, and nearly everyone attends."

"Not everyone." He glanced over to me, his arm brushing against mine. "Once every decade sounds like plenty to me."

"You're missing out," Miyu continued. "Rides, games, deep fried food, and cotton candy."

"That stuff is going to rot your teeth," Daxon replied.

I enjoyed this playful side of Daxon. As much as the new dark side of him turned me on, this version of him was much better when around other people. Though, I had noticed Rae had grown quieter the moment Daxon joined us. The alpha even made a joke that we were going on a double date, and when I reminded him this was more about Miyu wanting to see the fortune teller, he insisted a date was a date.

His hand slipped into mine, and well, there was no denying we were here as a couple. When I tripped over a tuft of grass, Daxon squeezed my arm and stopped me from falling face first into the grass. Blinking, I cursed myself for not watching out and becoming so clumsy lately. Though in all fairness, I had been caught up in how hot Daxon looked tonight...how tempting his full lips looked. So much so, that I had stopped paying attention to where I stepped.

"Would you prefer it if I carried you?" he teased, drawing me closer to his side. I rolled my eyes at him, and he threw his head back and laughed. The sound was like catnip to my vagina, or whatever the equivalent would be for a wolf.

I wondered which side was the real him? This laughing, smiling version, or the one that was a bit scary? I suspected it was more the broody half, which made me appreciate him even more for putting in such a huge effort on our double date.

"Normally, I can walk straight." I pinched my lips to

the side in a lopsided grin, and he laughed at me again, his hand squeezing my side as he tried to pull me even closer.

Leaning in close to me, he whispered, "You look beautiful tonight, sexiest girl I've ever seen."

I blushed all the way to the tips of my ears, even though the comment was relatively tame. I knew what that mouth was capable of. Miyu walked ahead of us, her and Rae hand in hand, chatting, and I was tempted to pull him into a dark corner for a moment and have my way with him.

"Though, you should have worn a skirt," Daxon told me.

I lifted my gaze to him, well aware of where he was going with his suggestion. "You don't like my skin-tight black jeans?"

His grin did things to me. Even on our way to the carnival, the way he studied me, his thumb circling the back of my hand with purpose, stirred an itch deep between my thighs. It was clear that the smallest thing set me off when it came to Daxon, and I gnawed on my lower lip to remind myself to hold on to some semblance of control.

When he leaned into me once more, a moan slipped past my lips, my nipples reacting, pushing against the fabric of my bra and the blue fitted top. "You have no fucking idea what they're doing to me." A long breath rushed from him and warmed my cheek. "I don't just want you, Rune. I need you."

I couldn't pull away from his side, and I once again found myself scanning the open land filled with shadows, wondering how easy it might be for us to sneak away for a quick kiss...or something so much more. Desire and logic waged a silent war within me, but with a single thought to the killer lingering in town, that fantasy was quickly resolved.

"Come on, we're falling behind," I said, dragging him by the arm, so we could catch up to Miyu and Rae, who were already at the entrance.

"Is that such a bad thing?"

I wanted to admit he had a point, but I refused to encourage him.

The closer we got to the carnival, the brighter the lights blinked and the quicker they chased away the night. Daxon bought us tickets, and once we walked in past the gate, I paused for a moment to take it all in.

Colored lights of every hue sparkled against the dark sky, laughter and music boomed in the air, and a strange excitement built up in my chest. I'd watched carnivals on TV shows, seen all the hidden kisses, the escapades, and the fun people always experienced at these places. With so much happening around me, I wanted to cry with joy that I had the chance to finally experience something normal. Sure, it might be lame to some, but to me, the tears pricking my eyes were real.

"Oh, where do we go first?" I asked, scanning the place with so many people and things to do. A Ferris wheel in the distance, the food trucks to the right, while straight ahead was a row of booths to win prizes.

"Your pick," Daxon muttered.

"The fortune teller perhaps," Miyu suggested hopefully.

That was when I spotted a nearby stand, overflowing with plush animal toys, and well, I naturally gravitated toward them. Not that I wanted one... Who was I kidding? I had to have one.

"Can we just try out one game at least first, please?"

"Of course," Daxon replied. "What Rune wants, she gets."

"I'm all for games over going to a psychic," Rae added, already guiding Miyu toward the stand I hurried toward.

"Yay!" Practically bouncing on my feet, I stood in front of a stand painted electric blue with an array of stuffed animals pinned around the edges of the booth.

"Are you good at throwing?" Miyu asked.

I shrugged. "Only one way to find out."

"What's the grand prize?" Rae asked, already eyeing the stacked up wooden bottles positioned along the back stand.

The man inside the booth pointed to an enormous striped llama attached to the inside upper corner, easily half the size of me.

"It's adorable," I said.

"All right, then it's a challenge." Daxon was suddenly next to me and paying the man. "A round of balls for each of us."

The man happily obliged and quickly set us up. All four of us were lined up with our own target, and I had no doubt that Daxon had a stronger throw than me. But he'd also told me the carnival was run by humans and that meant we had to be careful about showing off our strength. I picked up a leather ball that reminded me of a baseball, and a surge of confidence hit me. Miyu went first, managing to just skim the top bottle. I went second, hurling mine at the bottle. It hit it dead center, but bounced right off.

"What, no! Did you see that?" I protested. "Why didn't they fall?"

"You need more strength behind your throw, sweetheart," Daxon told me and tossed his ball with barely a look, completely missing the target...clearly doing it on purpose.

Daxon shifted to stand behind me, his body flush against my back, his groin pressed up against my ass, and he grabbed my hand with the new ball I'd picked up.

"Let's try this together," he whispered in my ear, which left me covered in goosebumps. How was I supposed to concentrate on anything when he rubbed himself against me like that, when his hot breath danced across my ear?

I glanced back at him. "If you keep doing that, neither of us will be throwing a ball for much longer."

"Is that a promise?" He brushed his lips across my earlobe. The next thing I knew, he hurled my hand and his forward, the ball slipping from my grip. It hit the top bottle, completely knocking it off.

"Yes!" I jumped up and down, thinking how amazing it was to find joy in the simple things.

Suddenly, Miyu squealed as she struck two bottles and they fell over. The guy congratulated her and handed her a small teddy bear from the wall as her prize.

"I'll do you one better," Daxon promised, and he grabbed a ball, then hurled it at his target with such strength that not only did he smash all the wooden bottles apart, but he'd managed to tear a hole through the back of the booth.

"Oh crap," I murmured.

As the guy turned to see what made the explosive sound, I quickly hurled my ball to distract him from the gaping hole, but my throw swung diagonally across the booth, bouncing off Rae's bottles and pitched right toward the guy's face. He cried out in terror, ducking, as Daxon thrust out his arm and caught the ball with ease.

"Holy shit, that was incredible!" I claimed.

Rae was hooting, while Miyu clapped. The guy handed us the huge llama, a disgruntled look all over his face. But technically, we had knocked over the bottles, so I grabbed my prize and hugged it against my chest before he noticed the gaping hole.

"Now that was fun," I said as we walked away. "Thanks for my prize."

Daxon flashed me a warm smile, offering a laugh. "You have a wicked curveball."

"She almost decapitated the guy with it," Miyu joked, giggling. "Okay, now let's go see the fortune teller."

"Maybe some rides first?" Rae asked.

"Babe," Miyu moaned in protest.

"I could do rides or the psychic," I whispered. "As long as we eventually get a corndog. I've always wanted to try one."

Daxon's lips pulled into an amused grin.

"Hope this isn't too boring for you?" I asked, genuinely worried he'd be bored to tears. Daxon was the opposite kind of guy who'd attend a carnival, as he admitted himself.

"Are you kidding?" he murmured softly. "To see you smile and watch your tight ass gives me plenty of time to work out the most creative way to rip your pants off of you later."

"You still owe me a new pair of leggings by the way," I teased, remembering how easily he tore them up with a single slice of his clawed hand. His destructive tendencies would probably destroy a lot more of my outfits if I let him.

I didn't really mind.

That time, Miyu must have heard our conversation, as she glanced over her shoulder at me with wriggling brows. I smirked back and lowered my head, loving that I had someone to talk to about guys and things in general. Miyu was incredible, and she was one of many reasons why I was beginning to want to remain in Amarok.

"Okay, we're going to the fortune teller first," she instructed.

We maneuvered through the crowds, and I couldn't remember the last time I smiled so much or enjoyed myself. When I noticed Daxon kept gazing my way, I said, "You're looking at me strangely."

"You don't want to know what I'm thinking," he delivered, his voice carrying hesitation.

"But I really do."

His gaze tracked my every step and movement, and that only left me blazing in heat. "I want you to have an incredible time. To keep wearing that sexy smile, to be by my side."

I eyed him. "Liar. That's not what you were thinking."

He arched one eyebrow casually, without any expression. "Correct." Not saying another word, he took my hand and dragged me past a line of people waiting to get onto the bumper cars.

Just then, we'd walked into a wave of people in our path, going in the opposite direction. Shoving and pushing me aside, Daxon's hand ripped free from mine.

I stumbled around, searching for a way out of the chaos, while someone trod on my foot, and another person whacked their hair in my face. I might have just found one downside to a carnival, and I pushed my way to the left when someone stepped into my path, and I literally walked into them.

Teetering backward, still gripping my llama plushy animal, I just wanted to get free. "Sorry." But when I looked up, I'd come face to face with Daniel. I hated how my first reaction was one of fear. I'd told myself I wouldn't let anyone push me around, but instinct had a mind of its own.

He gave me a dark look, and anger replaced the fear. Of course he would show up when I'd been having so much fun.

I should have turned away and merged into the crowd, but I didn't move.

"What do you want, Daniel?" I asked impatiently while rubbing my arms nervously down my sides.

"I know it was you who killed Eve," he hissed. "And I don't give a fuck what anyone else says. You don't have me fooled."

Stunned, I looked at him incredulously. "There was another murder, the poor man was killed the same way. And I have an alibi, so it couldn't have been me. I know you desperately want someone to blame for Eve, but it's not me."

He ignored me by the way his upper lip peeled over his row of white teeth.

"You never should have come to this town. No one wants you," he yelled at me, gaining the attention of several bystanders.

I swallowed hard, unsure how to make him see sense when he had made up his mind, when part of his mourning was tangled with hatred and revenge.

He closed the distance between us in one long step, and I threw my hands up against his chest to keep him away, but he leaned forward against my push. "I can't wait until everyone finds out the truth of the fucking monster you are."

A shadow fell over him, and he flinched back at the sight of Daxon.

"What the fuck do you think you're doing?" he growled out at Daniel. A deadly expression slashed over the alpha's face, one of twisted rage, of hostility, one that had me second-guessing the extent of how far he'd push his anger.

Daniel was backing away, his eyes flicking to Daxon, and his face had turned ghastly white. He was shaking his head, terror causing him to almost curl in on himself. "Nothing, I was just leaving."

Daxon's arm lashed out as fast as a viper's strike and grabbed the boy by the throat, hauling him back to him. "You think you have permission to talk to her? To so much as look at her?"

"I-I..." His eyes widened, and his mouth opened, but

no words came out. With anyone else, I might have enjoyed the intimidation show, except Daniel had lost himself to Eve's death. The poor guy trembled, and Eve would have never wanted to see him hurt. The way Daxon held him close, stared practically into his soul, I had no doubt he'd just scared the hell out of him.

"You and I have a problem," Daxon stated.

I shuffled closer, my pulse racing, and I placed a firm hand on his arm. "Please, just let him go. He's scared and grieving. He's going to leave me alone from now on, aren't you, Daniel?"

He nodded frantically.

Daxon didn't release him at first, but held him tighter, giving him the stare of death that would terrify anyone. "I rarely give second chances, but for Rune, you've earned yourself one favor. You owe her, but if I ever see you near her again, you won't even see me coming. Understand?"

Daniel half snorted a muffled, defeated cry.

Daxon released him, and Daniel whipped around, shoving into the crowd and vanishing in seconds.

"Shit, he was terrified," I said.

Daxon stepped up to me and cupped the sides of my face, studying my face. "Did he hurt you?"

"No, he's just angry and in pain from losing Eve."

"That doesn't warrant him blaming you, sweetheart. I heard him accusing you, and he's lucky I didn't rip his tongue out instantly. If he's smart, he'll keep the fuck away from you for good."

A shiver ran up my spine at the sincerity of his threat as I had no doubt he'd have hurt him if I wasn't there. Normally, I'd admit such protectiveness made me gush, but for Daniel, I couldn't help but feel pity. Maybe it was knowing that Eve adored him, so he couldn't be that bad, right?

Daxon drew me to him, and he kissed my brow. "It's my fault for losing you in the crowd."

"It's fine," I said and spotted Rae waving at us from near a large, purple tent. "Come on, let's go and have fun. I don't want to let this ruin the night."

"Agreed." His grip on my hand grew firm, and he carved a path for us through the crowd to reach my friend.

When we emerged, Rae and Miyu waited for us near the tent's entrance. Blinking Christmas lights ran around the frame of the tent, looking semi-festive. Above the doorway hung a sign with the words 'The Guardian Angel,' and I almost rolled my eyes at the name until I saw the excitement on Miyu's face.

"I've heard she's really good, and this year, I want to try her out," she said.

"You go, babe," Rae murmured. "I'll wait for you outside."

"I don't think so," she retorted, gripping her hips. "I've booked us all into a group session."

Daxon groaned behind me, and I grabbed his arm, then we followed Miyu and Rae inside. The llama in my arm proved problematic as it somehow wedged itself and me in the doorway of the tent. It took Daxon to tug on him to free me, and suddenly, I felt like one of those over-sized cats stuck in a dog door flap on the YouTube videos.

Bursting free, I stumbled into the tent, Daxon behind me setting the llama near the tent wall.

A single, flickering candle lit up the tent, filling the corners with shadows, casting light against a crystal ball sitting in the middle of a round table taking up most of the room. It was only the four of us, and I glanced around as Miyu took a seat, Rae doing the same.

"Are you sure you got the right time?" Daxon said. "Looks like no one's here, and this is probably a sign to not place your faith in hocus pocus."

Miyu looked slightly hurt by his comment, and my chest tightened as she had every right to believe in anything she wanted if it made her happy. And if wolf shifters like us existed, who said witchcraft and magic couldn't exist too?

"Come on, try and be open-minded," I muttered and took a seat alongside Miyu. It didn't take Daxon long to join us, and he flopped into the seat next to me. We all stared at the empty fifth chair, and I glanced around, not seeing another door leading into the place. Layers of fabric in various shades of purple and black covered the walls. A rusty looking chandelier dangled from overhead and appeared slightly tacky in an attempt to add some character to the tent. It failed miserably, along with the heavy scent of sandalwood incense.

Miyu was whispering to Rae, and her excitement had her bouncing her knees. It shook the whole table, even the crystal ball in its metal cradle.

"Will she be asking us questions?" Daxon's hand was suddenly on my thigh and inching up higher. My breath hitched at how quickly my body reacted to him. How a blaze kindled deep in my gut and dove to where my craving for Daxon awakened.

"Maybe," Miyu answered when it seemed I'd forgotten how to speak. "But you can ask her a question if you want. I figured we could do one where she just senses if there are any spirits around us, maybe they have messages for us from beyond."

Daxon's eyebrows shot upward with an overexaggerated response. "I'm not interested in what any of the dead have to say." He laughed at his own joke that none of us really got.

Rae sat back in his seat. "The quicker we get this over with, the better."

"Agreed," Daxon said, while his fingers inched higher still. I closed my thighs and stared at him, but he simply smirked evilly and pulled my thigh to the side, his hand quickly diving between them before I could respond.

His touch pressed against the seam of my heat, and despite it being over the fabric of my pants, it might as well have been skin to skin because he made sure I felt him. I squirmed in my seat, a moan slipping past my lips in response.

The way everyone looked at me left me mortified.

"Are you practicing for when the spirits arrive?" Rae teased, starting to make his own moaning sounds. I was certain my cheeks blushed as red as a tomato. Daxon just sat back, smirking his damn evil grin and enjoying himself.

Just then, part of the wall in front of us seemed to shift, and a figure emerged. A woman, maybe in her late thirties, joined us. She wore a purple corset that pushed up her ample breasts, along with a black skirt falling to her ankles. Her face was covered by a black lacy fabric, held in place by her hooded cape.

Hastily, I shifted in my seat and extracted Daxon's hand from between my legs, forcing it on the table, pressed underneath mine. Of course, I wanted his hand between my legs, but with everyone so close, I didn't want to be the person moaning randomly. Once was embarrassing enough.

"Welcome," she said, her voice playful, like she was used to the theatrics she put on for her clients. She was beautiful from what I could see through the material, with a heart-shaped face and large almond eyes, lips red as cherries. "I am Angel, and it's a blessing to read for you today. Take a few long breaths to clear out all negative thoughts."

She leaned across the table and collected the crystal ball, which she set aside on a nearby table, then picked up a deck of tarot cards.

Once she took a seat with us, she started shuffling the deck, never removing her veil, which intrigued me further.

"Tonight, we will use my cards," she instructed. "It's a lot easier in a smaller group like this." Her soft smile had a strange calming effect, and I figured this might be fun if nothing else. We were at a carnival after all, which wasn't meant to be taken seriously.

"Close your eyes and think about one thing you want answered," she asked, and I did as she asked, though my question came easily.

Will Alistair find me in Amarok?

The fact that my first question revolved around him

disappointed me, but I'd also been unable to get Sterling's appearance out of my head. I was surprised no one else had appeared. Maybe it was pure coincidence he'd found this town and me, and maybe word would never get back to Alistair that I'd been discovered.

"Once you're ready, open your eyes."

I opened my eyes, and in front of me on the table was a card, face down. There was a card in front of everyone else as well.

"Don't turn them over yet," Angel said just as Daxon did exactly that. "Oh, that's okay," she excused him. "We'll do you first.

We all leaned over to view his card, which depicted an old man in a long cape, holding a cane and lantern, looking down. It appeared rather depressing.

"The Hermit," Daxon said. "I don't think so. Let me pick another card." He leaned over, reaching for the deck, while the fortune teller quickly placed her hand over the pile.

"I'm sorry, that's not how this works. Each card was meant for you and brings a message just for you."

"What does his card say?" I asked, while the look on Daxon's face told everyone he wasn't happy with his selection. I got the impression he was a person who wanted only the best and always got his way.

Angel glanced down at his card for a long moment. "You're a quiet soul, and I sense you're hiding from your past, which makes it hard for you to get close to anyone. It's hard for you to connect with others."

Well, only that last part could be true, I guessed. I

didn't really think of Daxon as reserved or a quiet soul. Everyone noticed when he walked into a room.

Daxon didn't say a word, but his silence said it all. It only became more awkward as she kept going.

"You secretly want to be friends with everyone though, but you're afraid you won't be liked."

A snort slipped out of Rae at the ridiculous things the woman was saying. The more she talked, the more clear it was that she was making up crap.

"What do you see in his future?" I asked, sensing Daxon had no intention of asking any questions, and I felt bad for the poor woman. Daxon's hand fell back under the table and found the warmth of my leg, caressing me, distracting me.

"Loneliness," Angel answered, and Daxon licked his lips, shifting in his seat, and I could tell it took everything he had to hold back a smartass comment.

Angel picked up on his disinterest and pivoted her attention to Miyu next, while Daxon's hand squeezed my thigh slightly. He leaned in, his lips on my ear, whispering. "She has it wrong. I'll never be lonely because I'll never let you go. To keep you, I would sin, I would shed blood, I would die. Anything for you, sweetheart."

When he drew away, blood rushed to my head, my chest heaving for breath. His pupils dilated at watching my response, at how much I was falling over the edge for him. The things he said should have scared me, but instead, they made me shiver with a painful longing.

I must have lost myself in Daxon's gaze, at the way his fingers found the heat between my legs once again, because it took Miyu poking me in the shoulder to awaken me from the spell that Daxon had placed over me.

I twisted back to face Angel, who was staring at me, smiling. "Are you ready for your reading, dear?"

"Definitely," I said, clearing my throat and trying to get a hold of myself. It wasn't ideal to spend all of your time in a haze of lust.

She shut her eyes, and almost instantly, a chill fell over the room as if someone had switched on the air conditioner.

Suddenly, Angel slumped forward, the front of her head banging on the table so loudly, I jumped in my seat.

Miyu yelped, and Rae reared back in his chair. Daxon fell deadly silent, not even his chest moved with his breaths as he watched the fortune teller with intensity. Every inch of him screamed predator, and while the three of us backed away from something unknown, he was the kind to run to the monster.

"Fuck, is she dead?" Rae asked.

"Don't say that," I replied. "Maybe she's in a trance. One so powerful, she knocked herself out?"

Daxon snorted a laugh. "That would be hilarious if she did that, seeing she was full of shit."

Miyu leaned forward, a hand reaching for the woman.

"Not the best idea," Daxon warned.

"We need to know if she's okay. What if she's having a stroke or some kind of allergic reaction?"

"To what?" Rae asked. "Rune's reading?" He laughed, amusing himself.

"Well, when you say it like that, it doesn't sound good," I said.

It didn't stop Miyu, who poked the woman in the shoulder.

In a flash, Angel snapped back upright, and Miyu screamed. I flinched, my heart drumming in my chest as I tensed in my seat. Daxon never moved, he just tilted his head, watching her, and sniffing the air like he was searching for danger.

Something was wrong. "Why are her eyes white?" I murmured, and Miyu's gasp filled the silence.

Angel lifted an arm and pointed a long, slender finger in my direction. "Rune." The voice that came from Angel's lips did not belong to her. It sounded darker, deeper, and croaky, like it belonged to a much older woman.

"Monsters follow you in the shadows, but something darker, something more sinister resides within you. It will bring death and destruction to your feet. But you have the power to bring peace to the war you've unleashed. If you embrace it, what lies inside you will rule all."

Angel's words flatlined, and she fell forward, once more hitting the table with her head with such force, the whole thing shook.

"What the fuck was that?" My breaths came out in gasps.

"Damn, you got the best reading out of all of us," Miyu said, pouting, while I somehow suspected whatever we'd witnessed came from a place of truth.

Daxon was on his feet, and he took my hand. "We're leaving now." Before I could even check if Angel was all right, he grabbed my llama and whisked me out of the tent.

"I think that was real," I said while Daxon swiveled to stand in front of me.

"Everything about her was fake, and she put on a good show, that's all that happened. If she pretended to make yours appear real, then the rest of us would believe our readings."

I shook my head. "Did you see her white eyes, and she hadn't even turned over my card."

"Games. She smelled like just a human to me," Daxon said. "And we've wasted enough time there. I want to spend time with you alone."

He had a point on the theatrics of her reading. Rae and Miyu soon joined us.

"Is she alright?" I asked, to which my friend nodded. "Said she couldn't remember a thing and seemed to act like nothing strange happened."

"It was all a hoax," Rae added, to which Daxon nodded, though in my mind, it felt strangely real.

We all pushed into a walk, making our way to the Ferris wheel, when I slipped in next to Miyu. "Hey, did you tell Angel our names when you booked us in by any chance?"

"Nope, she insisted on not wanting to know anything about us."

A shiver crawled up my back. "Then how did she know my name?"

Miyu paused, grabbing my arm. "I told you she was fucking amazing."

That wasn't exactly what I'd call it, but whatever had

happened back in the tent left me covered in goose-bumps. Something was very odd, like her voice and basically everything she'd said about me. None of the others seemed particularly bothered about it though. Hmm.

Miyu curled her arm around mine and dragged me forward. "We may need another session at the salon to discuss the monster inside you." She giggled, and I felt kind of silly for taking anything that woman had said seriously. It was just a bit of fun from an obvious fake.

My life was already close to out of control, and I didn't want to accept that Angel's words were in any way a terrifying prediction.

"Hurry up, babe," Rae called out, holding the gate to the Ferris wheel ride.

We both rushed over. Her and Rae climbed into the first available passenger car, while Daxon looked to be getting us tickets from the side booth.

I hastily jumped into the next metal car as it swung down, figuring I'd grab it for Daxon and I, but just as I flopped down in the seat, someone else emerged from around the carriage and slipped into the seat with me.

I startled at first, until I saw who it was.

"Wilder?"

"Hello, gorgeous."

The man working on the ride hastily brought down the metal railing over us, and before I could even get my head straight that Wilder was at the carnival, we were moving upward, the carriage swinging under us.

I glanced over to Daxon, staring at us bewildered, his brow pinching, and under his arm was my stuffed llama. The situation wasn't helped one bit by Wilder waving down at him. Then he turned to look at me, and striking green eyes were all I saw, so bright, they could shine in the night.

"Daxon's going to be pissed you took his seat," I said, still surprised at Wilder's sudden appearance. Though my stomach fluttered at having his side pressed up against mine, his warmth like a blaze that heated me instantly, and when he placed an arm across the back of my seat, I naturally leaned in closer to him.

"I'm counting on it," he said. "Plus, he hates heights, so he can sit this one out."

"And I'm guessing you love them?" Each time the Ferris wheel moved and stopped, it sent us into a back and forth swing that left me feeling slightly dizzy.

"I've attended this carnival every year that it's visited town. I love any kind of ride." He leaned in closer. "And by the looks of it, the fair is agreeing with you too."

I pulled a face, then couldn't help but grin widely. "It's amazing. I can't remember the last time I laughed and had so much fun. Being serious is so overrated, and I could easily come here once a week to forget real life."

He laughed, the sound so beautiful to listen to that I'd gladly be in his arms as we swung around in the night air. We gradually inched upward with new people jumping into the passenger cars down below.

"How long have you been watching us?" I asked.

He raised an eyebrow and glanced down below to the expansive fair where people wandered around every-where. I could see the food vans, rides I definitely wanted to try next, and where there wasn't an insane amount of people. The vantage point was great for people watching.

"You'd be amazed how easy it is to find anyone from up here," he told me, his breath unexpectedly on the side of my neck. I turned toward him, only to find he leaned in so close, our lips and noses brushed.

"I can see that." My words expelled out as a breath.

That small innocent graze inflamed my desire and reminded me how the smallest touch drew us together. I felt the warmth of his fingers against my arm as they slid up to my shoulder and under my jawline.

I froze, thinking this wasn't the best place to get carried away. I tended to lose my head around Wilder... around both of them. The memory of the last time we'd had sex stirred my arousal though, and the movement of his arm around my back brought me closer to him.

Desire burned through my body, and I grabbed hold of his hand to stop him before it went too far, and I couldn't stop him...or myself. Goddess, I had become one of those girls, hadn't I? Where I was with two men, and no matter how much I told myself it would end in devastation, I couldn't back away.

I was too blinded by everything they made me feel, by them being constantly on my mind. I longed for another touch, for a kiss. They were my addiction. Even the way Wilder and Daxon looked at me unraveled me. They looked at me like they were starving. They looked at me like all they could think about was how to make me scream and the best ways to drag a climax out of me. How could I not be a goner around them? Fuck, they were ruining me. And even with my eyes wide open about where this all was heading, I begged for more.

We lurched upward once more, swinging as we

reached the twelve o'clock position on the wheel and halted for someone else to jump onto the Ferris wheel.

"You asked what I was doing at the carnival," Wilder said, his hand cupping my cheek, bringing me closer to him as he leaned in once more. "I came for you and only you. When I'm away, I feel an invisible pull to you, and the longer I'm away, the more insane I go."

I swallowed hard, unsure how to respond to that, but I didn't need to when his lips pressed against mine. He kissed me with passion, his tongue sweeping into my mouth, his hand behind my head, cradling me against him.

He bit down lightly on my lower lip, and I shivered underneath him as he slid his other hand under my top. I couldn't resist and leaned in to him, fisting his shirt, needing more. The heat from his chest consumed me, and it seemed to weave around me, keeping me captive to him.

His hand cupped the curve of my breast, his fingers finding the hardened nipple. I arched my spine, pushing close to him. He squeezed my nub to the point of pain, the most delicious kind of agony. My breath hitched along with a moan.

The approving growl in his throat did things to me, his domineering gesture affecting every fiber in my body.

Heat seared over my skin, and every nerve ending tingled.

My stomach fluttered as I'd never done this sort of thing in public with so many people around. Daxon was right down there. Thinking about him being so close had a crazy idea popping into my head that maybe he'd join us. I almost laughed out loud at the idea that two men who hated each other would ever cooperate in such a way.

It would be hot though. Probably the hottest thing ever.

At the end of the day, I understood the danger lurking in my decision to keep pushing my relationship with each of them. Because how could I pick between them?

But when his mouth slid over my cheek and found the softness of my neck, my thoughts flew away. I shuddered at his hot breath, the sexy groan on his throat.

"Fuck," he growled, his hand squeezing my breast harder. "I'm so close to losing all control, to stripping you right here and fucking you. I can smell your arousal, and I'm so hard that I'm dying for you."

I trembled at his words, moisture gathering between my thighs. I was finding it very hard to care about the people around us right now.

The carriage beneath us trembled as it lurched forward, sending us backward, dipping. Wilder broke from our kiss, his hand slipping out from my top, and he leaned back into his seat, smiling that wickedly sexy way he always did. Here I was, hanging high, desperate for more, but he just drew away.

My shoulders bunched up, and I stared at him incredulously. "I never took you for a tease," I said.

"Oh, gorgeous girl, tonight there are too many wolves around us, so that is all I can offer you." He looked at me innocently, like he hadn't planned this. Despite the flare of pleasure behind his eyes, he smiled, and I hadn't even noticed that we had started going around on the ride, as it was meant to be. His hand held mine on my lap, and a groan slipped past my lips.

"That's just cruel." I lowered my gaze to his lap, noticing the large tent in his jeans, knowing I wasn't the only one who would be starving tonight.

"Maybe I just want you to be thinking only of me all night." He smirked, and I knew that was the truth. I'm sure it had everything to do with Daxon. Wilder swooped in and staked his claim, and I'd fallen quickly. I groaned because he'd been right—after that small taste, I wouldn't be able to get him out of my head. All my attention focused on the way his thumb stroked my arm in small circles, bringing a flush across my skin.

"Just so you know, I'm not happy with this arrangement." Irritation jerked at my chest, but really, I could have said no. I turned my head and pretended to be mad.

"I can tell."

Asshole loved every second of leaving me hanging. His hand tightened over mine, and I couldn't believe how ravenous I was for him. The primal hunger flooded me again, a need I couldn't shake.

He smirked at me, and I felt pricks of desire dance between my thighs.

The Ferris wheel finally came to a halt, and the metal barrier keeping us locked in popped up.

Wilder climbed out, then offered me his hand, while with his other hand, he untucked his shirt to cover his erection. "Let's go, unless you want to go around again?"

Temptation swayed through me, but I eyed him, giving him my best evil expression, which only had him laughing. I was on my feet beside him in seconds, and when we walked out, Daxon stood there, still holding my llama, looking damn furious.

"Oh, look, it's Wilder," Miyu stated, her voice filled with more sarcasm than actual amazement. Rae was too busy staring at Daxon for a reaction.

"What the fuck are you doing here?" Daxon blurted and pushed the stuffed toy into my arms.

Wilder straightened his shoulders and stared right into his eyes, no hesitation. These two were about to go all alpha on us, and neither was going to back down first.

"I'm not fighting you tonight, so stand the fuck down," Wilder growled.

"Then fuck off. You're ruining my date with Rune."

Wilder glanced over at me, the skin around his eyes tightening, then he swung back to Daxon. "Then count me as your third wheel." He grinned wickedly.

I sighed at their macho show. I turned to Miyu, shaking my head. "Let's go on another ride while these two do their thing."

"Are you sure you don't want to watch?" Rae asked.

"Nope. I've seen enough of their aggression, and I want to enjoy the carnival before they tear down the place with their fighting."

*T*hese idiots were like fucking cockroaches I decided as I pounded the latest douchebag Rune's ex had sent. I'd found this one lurking right behind the restaurant, obviously having caught Rune's scent.

I'd made sure the first thing I did was to break the fucker's nose, but I wasn't sure even that would prevent him from being able to smell Rune. Her scent was...intoxicating.

And it seemed to be growing more so as the days passed.

I wasn't sure if that was because the mating bond was intensifying or because something was happening with her. But it was a bit concerning.

Because everyone else seemed to be noticing as well.

I'd even seen Marcus sniffing around her the other day, and he was hopelessly in love with his mate.

She just smelled that good.

"When's your alpha coming, big guy?" I asked as I

drove my brass knuckles into his gut. He moaned and coughed up some blood.

One thing was for sure, the guys coming were getting bigger. Of course that didn't mean they were any smarter. Obviously, Rune's ex valued force over brains.

Unfortunately for him and his men, I had both.

Another punch, this time a sucker punch in his mouth. I laughed as a few teeth fell out and he started bawling.

This was truly pathetic.

Protect our mate, my wolf growled. And I groaned because I knew what was going to happen next.

All my life, I'd been in perfect control of my wolf. Since our first shift, we'd existed in perfect harmony. Until now.

When it came to Rune, my wolf was batshit crazy. It was his world, and I was just living in it. I kind of was shocked every day that I woke up as a human because I kind of expected my wolf to take over, full moon be damned.

The bloodlust settled over my mind, and then there was nothing but the continued pounding of my fist hitting skin, destroying everything about this shifter who'd dared to come after our mate.

Protect.

A dark chuckle suddenly echoed through the alleyway. My wolf immediately recognized the asshole it belonged to.

Daxon.

"Well, look at this. What a pleasant surprise," he purred, stalking towards me. I turned my head and bared my teeth at him, my wolf not pleased at being interrupted. Not when we were trying to protect Rune.

"What did this poor guy do to you? He looks...terrible."

Daxon looked excited as he stared down at the huge guy crying at my feet.

I didn't explain myself to others. I especially didn't explain myself to Daxon.

But I had to admit this looked pretty bad.

"Look—" I began.

"Did that fuckwad ex of Rune's send him?" he growled, so much craziness in his gaze, even I felt a little scared at the sight.

Wait a minute... "You know about these guys."

There was a long pause, like Daxon was deciding something. "I've gotten rid of five so far," he admitted before launching a kick right at the midsection of the already ruined guy sniveling in front of us.

The crack of his ribs sounded through the alley, and Daxon and I both smiled.

"This is my third one," I told him, crouching down and lacing a rope embedded with silver around the guy's wrists with my glove protected hands. His whimpers increased as the silver began to burn through his wrist. They'd eventually burn all the way to the bone, and he'd have no relief until the rope was removed.

Unfortunately for him, the ropes were never going to be removed. Fortunately for him, he'd be dead soon.

"That's actually clever," Daxon said admiringly, crouching down next to me to inspect my handiwork.

"Don't sound so surprised, asshole," I growled, even as I hid a smile.

He smirked at me, his stupid golden boy smile on his face that never ceased to make me want to choke him.

Daxon tapped on the rope thoughtfully. "You make this yourself?" he asked.

"It comes in handy whenever I need to emphasize a point." I chuckled at the tame description.

"Hmm. I might have to borrow this idea," he said before standing up and scrutinizing me. "Maybe we have a little bit more in common than I thought."

I rolled my eyes. We both knew at one point, we'd thought of each other as closer than brothers.

The chasm between us seemed too wide to close at this point. There was a part of me that hated him more than any other person that existed. That part tended to block out anything inside of me that still considered him my brother.

"He's just going to keep sending them," I told Daxon as we continued to study the man at our feet.

Daxon's eyes glittered as he nodded. "I'm counting on that."

Daxon...was coming across a little bit like a psycho. What had he managed to hide from me and everyone else beneath that bullshit nice guy act that had always made me want to punch him?

"Eventually, he'll have to come himself," I said before bending down and grabbing the guy under his armpits to start heaving him away. Fuck, this guy really was a beast.

I should probably move the guy before anyone else from town happened to pass by though.

Although, part of me seriously doubted that Daxon just happened to find me. I'd felt Daxon watching me for weeks, ever since Rune had come into town. I'm sure he was trying to find out something he could use against me to get Rune all to himself.

Daxon surprised me by picking up the guy's feet and walking with me, a whistle on his lips that was possibly the creepiest thing I'd ever heard.

"Rune know you're creepy yet?" I taunted.

Daxon's grin just grew. "Maybe," he murmured, continuing to whistle.

We didn't say much as we walked, weaving behind buildings to avoid eyes. We were the alphas, there wouldn't be too many questions, but when there were eight dead guys between the two of us and Rune was already under suspicion by most of the town, it was best to stay as under the radar as possible when dragging a soon-to-be-dead guy.

I loved my pack, but I wouldn't put it past them to do something crazy like hand Rune over to one of the guys before Daxon and I could stop them.

And then I'd go crazy and probably destroy the entire pack.

So, I should do everything I could to prevent that.

I studied Daxon as we walked, noting the differences between his body language right now and how he usually was.

To the rest of the world, he was perfect. The perfect alpha, the perfect wolf, the perfect guy... I'd hated him for that, always felt compared, honestly.

I had my pack's loyalty, I didn't doubt that. But when

you were basically running a town with someone, it became a little more complicated than that. Daxon delighted in presenting himself as the good guy and leaving me to be the bad guy in most town decisions.

I resented him for that, but I guessed he also resented the fact that I'd ended up sleeping with his girlfriend, so we were perhaps even on that. Not that I'd known the reality of their relationship when it all went down.

Why was I thinking about that right now?

I shook my head to clear my thoughts, and Daxon smirked at me again, like he could read my mind. We were walking into the forest now. We probably should have been keeping an eye out for any shadow creatures, but between the two of us, there wasn't much we had to fear.

The guy's eyes opened just then, and they widened as he realized his predicament.

There was only one reason we'd be in the woods, and he knew it. He started to kick and scream, in general making a ruckus that echoed around us. Daxon promptly dropped the guy's legs and then pulled out a savage looking knife from his pants. He pried open the guy's mouth and sliced his tongue right off. I cringed as it flopped out to the forest floor.

I stared at Daxon in disbelief. He just smiled at me, almost angelically, like it was perfectly normal to slice someone's tongue off.

I mean, he'd told me he'd gotten rid of at least five of these guys already, but I'd envisioned it was how I'd done the job—a bullet to the head before burying them deep in the woods.

Now I was wondering.

The interloper had passed out from the pain, so I guessed at least we didn't have to worry about him alerting anyone anymore with his screams.

But it was going to take a while to get that image out of my head. I'd done a lot of things in my life, but chopping someone's tongue off wasn't one of them.

Daxon was watching me closely.

I cleared my throat. "Do that kind of thing often?" I asked, echoing his words from earlier. I kept my tone even, my mind remembering the kind of boy he'd been. The sunshine appearance of him hadn't been a mask back then. He'd freaked out on me if I accidentally squished an ant. Daxon had even tried to go vegan for a period of time, a practically impossible thing for a wolf, just because he couldn't bear to hurt another living thing.

I remembered noticing when he'd begun to use the golden façade more as a weapon than it actually being who he was though. And I'd never been quite sure what had brought about the change.

But the guy standing across from me...I suddenly wasn't sure if there was an ounce of that little kid in him anymore. He'd transformed, and somewhere along the way, I'd totally missed it.

"I'll do anything to protect her," Daxon announced fiercely. I could feel the promise behind his words. His "anything" literally meant *anything*.

But could he protect her from himself? And did he even need to?

Daxon picked up the guy's feet again, and we continued to march. I realized that I hadn't told Daxon where we were going, yet he was heading in precisely the right direction. The fucker really had been stalking me.

I shrugged it off for a moment, not in the mood to start another fight with him that would only inevitably draw attention at a time it was desperately not wanted.

Past the river, there was a piece of the forest that had always felt off. I'd heard townspeople talking about the place they never went to, even in wolf form. For centuries, they'd claimed this place was haunted.

A perfect place to store bodies.

Especially since it included a dramatic crack in the ground that seemed to descend forever. You couldn't see the bottom, even with a flashlight, and I wasn't about to see what else was down there.

I always got a jittery feeling here, an itching under my skin almost. Daxon looked completely at ease, however. The fucker was probably getting off on the feeling.

We dropped the guy on the ground almost simultaneously with a loud *thunk*, and he woke up. He stared at us with pleading eyes, an inhuman sound coming out of his mouth as he tried to beg for his life.

Guilt tried to flicker in my gut, as usual, but I pushed it away. This guy would have taken Rune away from me.

Mate, my wolf reminded me.

And I wasn't about to let that happen. Ever.

"Do you want to do the honor, or shall I?" asked Daxon, cocking his head and staring at me very animal-like. I could see his wolf in his eyes, waiting right beneath the surface for a chance to pounce.

"By all means," I said, kind of wanting to see this new Daxon in action. I felt like my whole world had suddenly changed, and I'd been let in on a secret of utmost importance.

Daxon grinned savagely, and I found myself grinning back, bloodlust leaking into my veins like I was breathing it in. I pulled out my gun to offer it to him, but he just waved it away. He knelt down behind the writhing picture of pathetic wretchedness and took out his blood-stained knife.

"You were stupid to come after what was mine," he said softly as he trailed the knife down the side of the guy's face, a line of blood forming.

My wolf growled that he'd dared to describe Rune as his, but I held him in check.

Without warning, Daxon suddenly stabbed the guy right in the throat. He then proceeded to pepper the guy's entire chest with stabs before finally ending the guy's life with a sharp stab to the head.

Holy freaking hell.

Daxon stood up, his eyes dilated like he was high. He staggered a little bit, a moony grin on his face.

All right, I was officially in the presence of a crazy person. I kicked the dead guy into the jagged crevice, not listening for the body to hit the bottom. It was so deep, I never did.

I warily watched Daxon, making sure he didn't suddenly jump me. But he was busy wiping down his knife and whistling again.

After he was finished, he tucked the knife back in his pocket and began to walk back the way we'd come, somehow not having a drop of blood on him.

"Let me know if you find any more wanderers," Daxon said. "And I'll do the same for you."

"I appreciate the help," I answered after a long pause. It was kind of weird to be actually getting along with him.

"Anything for Rune," Daxon said softly, his words an echo of his earlier statement. "And when the asshole finally comes, we'll be ready for him."

A thrill of anticipation, and foreboding, flooded over me.

"We'll be ready," I agreed as we made our way out of the woods.

Daxon was most definitely deranged, but I guessed as long as he used his evilness for Rune, I could work with that.

A small part of me was a little bit happy to have a moment of peace with him as well after so many years of fighting.

I'd never admit that though.

Rune

THE MOON GODDESS called to me. I could feel her as I sat up in the bed and looked out the window to where the full moon streamed in. I got up, as if in a trance, and pulled on some shorts before stumbling out of my room, down the stairs, and out the back door. I walked barefoot until I found myself standing by the river.

I craned my neck backwards, desperation to feel as much of her light as possible soaring through my veins. I soaked the moonlight in, welcoming it with every piece of my soul.

I blamed her for Alistair and the state of my life, but I couldn't resist her call.

I scrunched my toes in the mud of the riverbank, soaking in the coolness of the soil against my skin. I took a step closer to the water, allowing it to lick at my feet. It felt like I was being energized from above and from below, the moon goddess sending her power through her light and the earth grounding me from below.

Something leaped in my chest, and I grabbed at it. It happened again and again, until I was sure that I was having some type of heart attack. I sank to my knees as some force rushed over my body until I was bending forward, bowing down to the goddess and her reflection in the river.

Pulse after pulse of power—that was the only way to describe it—flowed over me. My breath came out in short gasps as my fingers dug into the dirt, trying to withstand whatever was happening.

I ripped my head up towards the heavens and let out an inhuman scream at the sky. The sound was threaded with its own pulse of power. I screamed at the heavens. My scream carried all the things I never said out loud.

Like how much I hated her for linking my soul to someone who wouldn't treasure it like she'd promised it would be treasured.

Like how much I hated her for taking away my mother.

Like how much I hated her for allowing my wolf to be taken from me.

It was that thought that did it. As if I was being burned alive from the inside, fire roared through me, singeing every single bit of my insides until I was sure there was nothing left but ash.

My shoulder screamed in agony, right in the place where I'd been branded on that fateful night so long ago. The fire licked through me, centering on that one spot, until black spots began to dance across my vision. I was about to pass out when the pain abruptly disappeared, leaving me breathless and sweating. The pressure that had been beating against me was gone as well, and I rolled my shoulders back, trying to get ahold of myself.

I felt so...strange. Light almost. Like a burden I hadn't even known I was carrying had suddenly disappeared. How had I existed like that this whole time? How had I not known what I was dragging along with me?

I stood up on shaky legs, feeling like I could fly. Like I'd become so light that at any moment, my body was just going to soar up into the heavens because there wasn't anything to keep it down anymore.

A giggle exploded from my throat, the sound so light and carefree that I didn't recognize it. I laughed again, and a tear slid down my face at how freaking good it felt.

The sound was abruptly cut off as a crack sliced through my back, hunching me forward as something in my chest expanded outwards. Excruciating pain sliced through me, and I screamed as every bone in my body seemed to break at once. The pain lasted for what seemed like an eternity until suddenly, it was gone, and I found myself looking at a world that had been remade and out of eyes that I didn't recognize.

It took me far too long to realize what had happened to me, because it was something that I hadn't even dared to dream about.

I had shifted. My wolf and I were finally meeting.

Hello, my heart murmured to her, and I felt her love wash over me, her happiness that she was finally free.

Hello my friend, her voice whispered back to me. If I were human, I would have cried from the happiness I was feeling... Maybe euphoria was a better term for this actually.

I dashed to the river's edge, desperate to see myself, even if I stumbled over my own paws. How did one coordinate walking on all fours anyway? I whimpered when I saw an arctic white wolf staring back at me from the water's reflection, silver threads seemingly woven throughout my coat like the moonlight was peeking out and my same blue eyes peering at me. I looked down at my paws, admiring the fact that they were a majestic silvery color. I'd never seen a wolf with silver feet before. I picked up my right front paw and cocked my head as I examined it closely. My fur was practically glittering. That was freaking cool.

We're beautiful, I thought to myself.

Damn right, my wolf agreed.

My head shot back, and my wolf let out a howl that surely reached the moon goddess herself. It was laced with freedom and thankfulness...and joy. I didn't know how this had happened, but I rejoiced in the fact that my wolf was finally with me. That I could finally be who I was always meant to be.

And then I was off, my wolf desperate to run, to feel

the wind through her fur, to experience what we'd both been missing. The breeze danced through our fur, and I wondered how shifters didn't do everything they could to stay in their wolf form and experience this.

Everything around us was magnified, our sight clearer and crisper, our nose almost overwhelmed with all the new scents around me, our hearing discovering a cacophony of sounds that blanketed the air around me.

How could I go back after this to a reality where I knew this all existed, but where I couldn't experience any of it? Maybe I'd just stay a wolf forever.

My wolf snorted at my dramatics.

A branch broke behind me, and I whirled around, my teeth bared as I searched my surroundings for any threat. I got distracted though when I saw my footprints in the ground behind me, illuminated clearly under the moon-light because they looked like they'd been sprinkled with silver glitter. I watched as the wind blew through and the footprints disappeared as the silver imprint was carried away like ash in the wind.

Well, I hadn't ever heard of that before.

A branch creaked again, and my attention was temporarily diverted from the strange sight. My wolf sat back on her haunches when a rabbit timidly made its way out of the underbrush.

Dinner.

I launched myself at the unsuspecting creature, grab-bing its neck in my mouth as I yanked my head back and forth to break its neck.

Not sure how I knew how to do that, but I guessed it

was instinct. I gulped the rabbit down in what seemed like one bite, and then my wolf was off.

And this time, she kept running. So fast that the world literally melted around us, looking nothing but a blur. At times, she would slow down and I would see unfamiliar canyons and ravines and untraveled roads. I was in the background while she moved, a passenger just along for the ride. I wanted to run forever, to feel this peace where I allowed instinct to take over without care for anything else that existed in the world.

We dashed up the side of a mountain, every step landing smoothly and gracefully in a complicated dance I knew I'd never have been able to accomplish in my human form. We reached the peak where the entire world seemed to be laid out in front of us, and then my wolf crouched down...and we jumped.

I woke up with a gasp, my hands clawing at the sheets desperately as that roller coaster like feeling faded away. I wasn't falling. I was in my room, in the inn.

My heart was threatening to break out of my chest, and I stared at the ceiling and counted the tiny cracks I saw as I tried to calm down.

Just a dream.

It was just a dream.

If it was just a dream, it would explain why I felt like I was dying. Like something had been taken away from me. Disappointment was an understatement for how I was feeling as I collected the pieces of the dream that I could remember.

I'd dreamed I'd shifted. I didn't know whether I was grateful that I'd gotten to experience my wolf for a second in my sleep, or if I was devastated because it just pushed the knife in more now that I was back in reality and without her.

"Shit," I whispered as I finally sat back and went to wipe the sweat off my forehead with the back of my hand. Except right before I did, I noticed that my hand was streaked with dirt. I stared at it, uncomprehending how that had gotten there. I slid from my bed when I realized that all of my sheets were covered in dirt, along with my arms and my clothes and my feet.

A fluttering feeling gnawed at me when I saw something furry and bloody at the end of my bed.

It was a dead rabbit, obviously half eaten.

Well fuck.

What the hell had happened to me last night?

*A*fter having a slight mental breakdown and trying unsuccessfully and desperately for an hour to shift, I finally showered the mud off my body and gave the sheets on my bed to housekeeping. The bunny was tossed out the window. It didn't look in the least bit delicious now that I wasn't a wolf.

Please come back, I cried silently, staring at my hands and willing them to change somehow. I'd grown up believing that I was Lycan, and it was no longer a full moon, but a girl could dream, right? Especially after the extraordinary circumstances of my maybe shift. I still wasn't all the way convinced that it had actually happened. Pawprints made of silver dust that drifted away in the breeze? That was...unique.

I paced back and forth across my room before deciding that I needed to talk to Daxon or Wilder or both about what I thought had happened the night before. They might think I'd gone insane, but I'd run that risk. I was about to go insane if I didn't share this with someone soon.

I marched out of the inn and down the street, not exactly sure where I could find either of them at this time of day. They kind of always found me, seemingly having some kind of Rune tracker they used to locate me no matter where I was. I should probably get a cell phone one of these days. I got nervous every time I thought of getting one though, like Alistair could somehow track me down, even with a new one.

"Rune," Miyu suddenly yelled. She was coming out of Mr. Jones' coffee shop, and I smiled and waved at her, glad she already had her coffee. I was going to have to return there sometime, the pastries and drinks were way too good, but for now, I was content wallowing in my embarrassment without Mr. Jones' all-knowing eyes watching me. Plus, I would have to remember to always go with some kind of taste tester or at least someone who could yell at me if I lost my head and agreed to drink one of his concoctions once again.

"I was about to track you down at the inn," she gushed with a huge smile. I cocked my head and studied her. Miyu looked different, like she was glowing almost.

"I have something huge to tell you, and it's all thanks to you," she continued, taking my arm and dragging me towards her salon.

"Ok, what is it?" I asked the second the salon door had shut behind us. Her enthusiasm was contagious, pushing aside all of my confused thoughts about last night. Well, almost pushing away all my thoughts.

"Rae and I are going to have a mating ceremony," she

squealed, jumping up and down and squeezing both of my hands.

"You are?" I breathed, my initial shock fading away into excitement for my friend. Mating ceremonies weren't necessarily required, the whole biting the other person was the only thing you ever needed, but it was a beautiful way to celebrate a couple's decision. Kind of like the humans' wedding, it gave everyone the chance to congratulate the newly mated couple.

"When are you having the ceremony?" I asked, a pang settling through me as I really thought about it. I was beyond happy for Miyu that she was taking the leap, I really was. But it made me think of what should have been. As the alpha's true mate, Alistair and I should have had a huge celebration. I shook the thought away and concentrated on Miyu.

"Next week," she squealed.

I gaped at her. That was quick.

"I made him wait long enough, I decided that I wouldn't wait to make him do the ceremony. And my mom has basically been planning my mating ceremony since the day I was born, so there's actually not too much to plan," she said with a snicker. "I was going to ask though... I don't have very many friends here, no real reason why, I've just never really connected with anyone. Until you. Will you be one of the girls to stand beside me on the big day?"

My heart hitched, and there was a scratchy feeling behind my eyes as I tried not to cry. "Really?" I cried, throwing my arms around her.

She let out a sob, and then I was sobbing. We would

probably look like crazy people if anyone were to peer in through the salon's windows. But I didn't care. This was one of the best things to ever happen to me. Before I'd come here, I never would have even dreamed of having a friend, let alone a close enough friend to ask me to participate in the mating ceremony.

"And don't worry," she purred, "I'm not going to have you wear something ugly. All of my girls are going to look like babes standing next to me."

I chuckled and finally let go of the death grip I had going around her waist. We both wiped our eyes and stared at each other before Miyu started jumping around the room. "I'm so excited," she crowed.

I couldn't help but laugh, the happiness bubbling out of me.

Once we'd jumped around and rocked out to a new song she was loving from a band called Sounds of Us, we settled into the chairs she had set up for guests.

"Oh, I'm a terrible friend," she suddenly said.

I looked at her, confused.

"When I saw you walking down the sidewalk, you looked really upset. I was going to ask you about it, and then of course I got distracted by telling you the news."

I bit my lip, wondering if I should even say something right now. I really just wanted to be normal for a minute, but I also was desperate to talk about the fact I may have actually shifted last night. Miyu knew that I couldn't shift, and that it had something to do with my ex, but we'd never talked about it extensively. It was kind of a tough subject obviously.

"Tell me," she coaxed, her soft eyes telling me I was in a safe place.

"Something happened last night. I...think I might have shifted," I told her.

Her eyes widened. "What?"

I suddenly felt really insecure. What if everyone thought I'd been lying all this time once they found out, and I became even more a suspect in Eve's death, because they thought I was a murderer?

Worthless little bitch. Alistair's voice sang through my head, and I pushed him out. This was the new version of myself. I could trust. I could take chances. I could do it.

I proceeded to tell her everything I remembered. Her eyes widened even further as I talked, until she kind of resembled one of those cartoon people with humongous eyes.

I went on and on until I finally collapsed back against my seat, feeling overwhelmed and tired.

"Rune Celeste Esmeray, I knew you were going to bring adventure into my life the second I saw you," she said thoughtfully. "I know what we need to do. We need to go to the pack library."

She stood up and began to march towards the door like it had already been decided.

"Wait...what?" I asked. "You want to go to the library?"

"This isn't your average library, babe," she explained, ushering me out of the salon, and I reluctantly headed outside. "From the time the town was first created, the alphas have been collecting whatever shifter books they could find. We probably have one of the best libraries in the world honestly. Daxon and Wilder have only made it better during their tenures."

I couldn't help but look up and down the street for them when she said their names, kind of surprised they hadn't popped up yet. Maybe they thought I needed some girl time. And I did, I didn't want to become one of those girls who couldn't exist without their guys for more than a minute...but it was getting hard.

"You've got it bad," teased Miyu. I growled at her in response, and we both looked at each other shocked. I'd been doing that more and more lately, a decidedly un-Rune-like trait prior to coming to this town.

You did a lot of growling and howling last night, a voice in my head reminded me.

Miyu led me to a side of town I hadn't really explored yet. There was an enormous red brick building with white Corinthian columns tucked away on the far east side of town. It had three sets of double doors in front and definitely looked every inch the impressive library I'd been picturing in my mind. I wasn't sure how I'd missed this. I was obsessed with books.

"So what do you think we'll find here?" I asked as she led me through the center doors. I gasped when we got inside. The doors opened to an enormous room that was open in the middle. Shelves of books lined the walls and more shelves were lined up in rows in the middle of the room. The open ceiling showcased another three stories, where the walls were lined with shelves of books, wrought iron railing separating them from the levels below. Above all of that, looking down at the open floor like a benevolent god, was the most beautiful stained-glass window stretching almost the entire width of the ceiling. Glass panels stained with seemingly every color in the rainbow made up a multitude of different murals and scenes. I'd never seen anything like it. I gaped at it for a second, trying to absorb everything depicted on it, but Miyu was already dragging me forward.

Like any good library, it was silent, and I only saw a few people milling around.

In short, I'd found where I was going to be spending my days when I wasn't working. This was the perfect place to hide from unwelcoming townspeople and feed my addiction of reading. It would take a million shifter lifetimes to be able to read all of these books.

I was up for the challenge.

"Amazing, right?" Miyu asked, an amused smirk on her lips as she watched me absorb our heavenly surroundings.

"Amazing," I repeated back softly.

A stern-faced librarian gave us suspicious looks as we passed like she was worried we were going to abscond with the books...or maybe she doubted we read. Either way, I forgot her as Miyu led me deeper into the library.

"In answer to your previous question," Miyu began, "there's got to be some kind of book in here that talks about what happened to you. Or even talks about wolves that looked like you in shifter history. I mean, I've never heard of a white and silver wolf that left glitter pawprints behind them."

I snorted at how ridiculous it sounded, but it really was how I remembered it. She went to a section entitled 'Famous Shifters' and grabbed a bunch of random books.

I grabbed some as well, and then we made our way to a table hidden behind some of the shelves.

"I don't know much about being a good researcher, but I'm going to give it my best," she told me, and the girl stole my heart once again. Here we were, a week out from her last-minute mating ceremony, and she was here in the library determined to help me.

Best friends forever status right there.

We spent the next few hours pouring through the books, finding out a lot of really interesting things about wolves I'd never heard of but not discovering anything that seemed similar to what had happened to me.

"Shit," Miyu suddenly said, "We've been here for four hours. I have to go to the motherfucking cake tasting."

"Why is that a motherfucking kind of appointment?" I asked wryly, stretching my arms above my head and realizing from the late shadows that were coming in from the window above us how much time had passed.

"Because Rae likes vanilla and I like chocolate, and before you say that we should have both, just know that this cake place has like twenty different cake flavors, so just imagine how amazing this cake could be if it weren't for my killjoy groom."

I snorted and shook my head, and she gave me a sly wink. "Get out of here. I'll put the books back when I'm done. I think I'm going to stay a little longer," I told her.

She gave me her signature beaming smile.

"And thanks," I told her softly, hoping she understood just how much I was thanking her for.

"Of course, Rune. You're not alone anymore," she responded before beginning to walk away.

"And dress fittings are on Wednesday at five," she practically yelled over her shoulder, eliciting a loud "Shh" from the librarian we'd encountered when we'd first walked in. Miyu's answering giggle seemed to somehow fill up the entire enormous room as she disappeared from sight.

And then it was just me and a million books.

I spent another hour looking through the pile of books we'd chosen before deciding to peruse the stacks for more. I made my way down row after row, my gaze catching on a never-ending number of books I wanted to read later...like when I had my life figured out.

I was about to give up for the day when my eyes came across a book called *Curses and the Forbidden Arts*. Well, that kind of sounded promising, especially after what Alistair had done to me.

I picked up the book and settled back into my seat at my table. Flipping through the pages, my eyes widened as I read about all the terrible crap someone could do to you. Everything sounded so complicated as well. How did Alistair's pack know how to do these kinds of things in the first place?

I finally flipped to a page entitled "*Shakranda*." That was the curse that Wilder had mentioned to me at one point that he thought had been done to me. I read through the page, my heart picking up speed as I read through a very familiar description. Yep, this sounded exactly like what had been done to me. Alistair was a fucking bastard.

I got to the end of the page though, where it read, "The *Shakranda* is unbreakable to anyone but the original caster of the curse. It is impossible to lift the curse with any other means."

I set the book down and blew some hair out of my face, my thoughts in a whirl. If Alistair really did have the *Shakranda* placed on me, then something really weird had happened last night. And even if I couldn't figure out how to shift in the light of day, something told me that the curse had definitely been broken last night.

It was official—I was a freak. And something definitely strange was going on with me.

I was going to be living in the library for the time being until I found something out. I hoped that lady at the front would be okay with that.

13

"Burger, no tomato, and extra pickles," the man at the booth ordered, his eyes still glued to the menu like he had more to order, while his wife sipped on her Coke through a straw, staring up at me like I was a freak. I'd noticed lately more people coming into the diner spending their time watching me. I wasn't sure if it was related to the murders or the fact that the whole town seemed to be buzzing with news that I was spending so much of my time with both Wilder and Daxon. Though, I hoped it was the latter since the majority of locals had accepted I couldn't be the murderer after word spread I had both men in my room during Asher's attack.

That I guessed was where the gossip had started.

"And a side of fries." The man stuck out the menu at me, then looked over to his wife, who popped the straw out of her mouth. "Caesar salad, doll." She handed me the menu too, but didn't let go when I grabbed it. "I'm curious, what's it like being with two alphas at once? Do you enjoy seeing them fight over you? You know, we're all taking bets on how long before you break them...just like Arcadia."

My shoulders reared back, her comment taking me off guard. I stared at her grin while a rush of anger filled my veins. "Are you serious?" I snatched the menu from her hand, stunned that she so blatantly said that. And were people really taking bets on us?

"For fuck's sake, Narell," the man said on a groan. "You want her to spit in our food? At least ask her after we get our meals." The awkward fake smile he gave me offered no consolation.

I huffed and marched back toward the kitchen, hearing them bickering behind me. What assholes. I stepped into the kitchen and slammed the door behind me, then sucked in shaky breaths, the menus shaking in my grip.

"How the fuck is it their business?" I mumbled under my breath, hating that people were gossiping about us but kind of understanding it too. Wilder and Daxon were both larger than life figures in this town. Of course, everyone would want to know everything about them.

"You all right?" Rae asked, and when I looked up, he was holding a sack of potatoes, which he proceeded to dump on the counter near the sink. His hair was pinned in a net, his apron covered in dirt from the sack.

"A customer just told me that people are taking bets on how long before I drive Wilder and Daxon crazy like their ex. Can you believe that?"

He dumped some of the potatoes into the sink. "Don't pay them any attention. Most people in this town are bored out of their heads, and they would be entertained by a turtle race if it gave them something to talk about. Either that or they're jealous as fuck, wishing they could be in your position."

I pinched my lips to the side, still annoyed by her comment.

"Did you know I get all my gossip from a ketchup bottle?" Rae said, catching me off guard, and I glanced up at him, confused by his comment.

He took my confused look as an okay to respond.

"It's a very reliable sauce." He chuckled to himself as he started washing the potatoes.

"Your jokes are getting worse," I teased. "But at least that one made me smile."

"Then my job here is done." He started humming to himself, and I gave him the order I'd just received.

Once in the main diner, I set the menus back into the holder on the front counter, scanning the tables for dirty dishes to collect, any refills needed, or anyone trying to grab my attention. It was a quiet day with only half a dozen customers, so I was managing the floor alone.

The front door bell chimed, and I turned around to greet the customer, but instead, my gaze lifted to meet Wilder's. My heart fluttered in my chest at his arrival, having no idea why he'd visited, but it did the trick of dissolving the woman's words from my mind. Wearing a checkered button-up shirt, with his large build and those powerful biceps, he looked every bit a rugged cowboy. His jeans hung low, his silver belt buckle glinting against the light pouring in from outside, and it took every inch of strength to not throw myself into his arms.

"Hey, gorgeous," he said, leaning in and stealing a kiss, ignoring everyone else around us. I could feel all the busybodies watching. I felt their stares on my back, but maybe it was worth giving them a show rather than pretending nothing was happening with Wilder and I.

Stepping closer, I cupped his face and kissed him hard, a warm feeling spreading from my chest all the way down to my toes. The delicious sweet taste of him flowed into me, seeping deep into my bones. He'd just walked into the diner and I had seen him yesterday, yet I was clinging to him, drawing him closer, ensuring he knew how much I missed him. I pressed my breasts against him.

The sharp ding of the kitchen bell broke through the spell, and I drew back, licking my lips. "It's great to see you," I said. "Why are you here?"

"I'm hungry," he admitted, and his features softened. "Plus, I wanted to see you. I sure hope I'm the only customer who receives that sexy welcome."

The bell rang again, and an urgency raced up the back of my legs to serve the finished meal. Quickly, I grabbed a menu and said, "Don't you know it." I winked, then turned and waved for him to follow. "This way." My voice had been louder than I'd intended.

I guided Wilder to the booth near the bar area and away from the other customers in the diner, not wanting them anywhere near to hear us. "I'll be right back."

I darted to the kitchen window and collected the first two plates for table four. As I delivered them, I noticed the two older men starting at me strangely. Had they bet on me? I hoped they lost every last cent.

Despite their wry expressions, I delivered a gloriously happy grin. "Hope you enjoy your meals."

Then I made my way back to Wilder, unable to keep away from him. Overhead, a slow pop song played I hadn't heard before, and as I paused near his booth, my toe tapped to the tune.

"Have you decided what you're having?" I asked, watching the way he folded up the sleeves of his shirt to his elbows, my attention fixated on his powerful forearms, his muscles and sun-kissed skin, but most of all, thinking about how incredible it felt to be wrapped in them.

"Ribeye steak, rare, with grilled vegetables."

"You know Rae makes the meanest steak in town, so good choice." I reached down to collect his menu, and he took my hand in his, his touch lingering, sending jolts of excited shivers up my arm. "And for dessert, you can take your break." His grin was pure evil, and my mouth opened with a response, but the words remained stuck in my throat.

I didn't have anything to say, since I had no problem being his dessert. He was my temptation, and I couldn't help but wonder if he came to the diner for the purpose of reminding me how weak he made me around him.

"Bring the chocolate sauce too," he whispered, and something inside me flared, something so deep and explosive that I found myself clenching my thighs at his offer.

"I-I'm alone serving today, I can't leave Rae alone. But maybe later?" I chewed on my lower lip, my mind desperate to know more about Wilder, me, and the chocolate sauce.

He laughed, making that hypnotic sound that had my knees shivering. When the kitchen bell chimed again, I sighed that I was being called from Wilder's side. And I didn't move at first, unable to get my legs to move when I wanted everything he promised me.

"If you keep staring at me like that, I'll be enjoying you as my dessert right here on this table."

My pulse skipped a beat as images flooded my mind, of me naked and lying on the table before Wilder, his hands forcing my legs wide as his mouth devoured me. I shivered thinking of the possibilities. I was driving myself mad with desire.

What was happening between Wilder and me, even Daxon and me, came down to pure chemistry. The kind that felt like it might explode inside me if I did nothing about it.

"It's so hot in here," I said, letting my thoughts spill out, gaining myself a gorgeous grin from Wilder. My cue to go and do my job came with the next ring of the bell from Rae, who seemed very impatient all of a sudden. "I'll be back."

Swerving around, I made a mad rush across the diner, noting a couple waited by the cash register to pay.

"I hope you enjoyed your meals today," I said as I punched in their bill, easily remembering what everyone ordered. After collecting their payment and thanking them, I rushed to collect the next plates. I was so distracted by Wilder's comments that it didn't even bother me when I delivered them to the gossiping couple.

"Enjoy your meal," I said, sliding their plates in front of them, smiling and quickly turning from them.

"Hmm, there's no ketchup on the burger," the man said.

With the earlier frustration rising once more in me, I collected the bottle of ketchup from a nearby table and brought it to him. "Here you go, sir," I answered through clenched teeth, noting his wife studying me with a strange look.

"I don't blame you," she whispered, then glanced over her booth to where Wilder sat at the end of the room, and then back at me. "Every woman would kill for a night with him."

Her husband didn't seem to hear and was already biting in his burger, sauce dripping down his hands.

I had no words and didn't want to encourage the flames of gossip, so I gave her a slight nod and returned to clean the table from the couple that just left.

By the time I finished, my breaths were ragged, but I patted down my hair and quickly removed my apron as I made my way back to Wilder, finding myself putting an extra swing in my hips.

"Hi there," I said, aware that his presence was making me act stupid.

"Been watching you," he said, leaning an arm on the booth behind him, half twisting in my direction. "At how much your ass wriggles when you're bent over the table, wiping it down." His gaze blazed over me, and that earlier heat now shot right to my cheeks. Only when I spotted the gossiping woman wrenching her head back to look at us did I realize I'd completely forgotten to put his order in with Rae.

Crap. What was wrong with me today?

"Hold that thought." I whipped around and rushed into the kitchen, drawing in fast breaths, my heart going a million miles an hour.

"Ribeye, rare, grilled veggies for table seven," I puffed out the words.

Rae gazed at me with hooded eyes. "Girl, you're so transparent, even the Martians could see how much you're lusting over Wilder."

I stiffened. "What are you talking about? It's hard being out there on my own."

He folded his arms across his chest. "You're not fooling anyone, but the guy is into you. You don't even need to try."

I blew out a long sigh. "I get so hot and nervous around him, which is stupid." I headed to the fridge and opened it, then bathed in its coolness for a few moments.

Rae laughed at me. "Miyu was the same when we first met. She tripped over her own feet, forgot how to speak sometimes, and that's when I knew she was the one for me."

He could have been talking about me right then and the way I'd been acting around both Wilder and Daxon, but did that make them the ones for me?

"You better get back out there," Rae said, and I grabbed a cold bottle of water, a glass from the rack, and headed out to where more customers had entered the diner. I delivered the water to Wilder and got back to work.

The next couple of hours were a blur of customers coming and going, and as much as I wished I could have spent more time with Wilder, that wasn't possible. He watched me the whole time though. I'd never imagined having someone looking at me could be such a confidence booster. Usually, I was trying to run away from attention.

By the time I finally collapsed in a seat to rest, only one customer remained and even Wilder had gone into his office in the back, saying something about paperwork.

"Why did I agree to work a shift on my own again?" I murmured to myself.

In that same moment, Licia and Marcus waltzed into the diner, both of them co-owners of Moonstruck Diner along with Wilder.

Right behind them, Daxon stepped inside too, and I instantly straightened at his arrival. Suddenly, the air in the diner thinned and my heart raced. He wore a black leather jacket over a black shirt and dusty blue jeans that hugged his strong thighs. His wind-blown hair framed his handsome face. To say his presence left me overwhelmed in emotions was an understatement. He was a freaking god.

He scanned the place, and then his gaze settled on me. His smile brightened everything, and he strutted over to where I sat, his attention sliding up and down my body. Every part of me tingled with excitement. Wide shoulders tapered down to a narrow waist. He moved more like a lion than a wolf, silent and powerful.

I was on my feet as he reached my side, smiling. "Hey,

gorgeous. I was hoping to find you here. I want you to come with me," he stated without pause.

"Where to?"

"I want to take you to a lookout nearby before we have to be at Miyu's wedding. It's the best place to watch the sunset around here." His fingers reached over and curled around my hand, my fierce infatuation with him consuming me.

He tugged me closer to him, and I stumbled on my feet, savoring the way his breath washed over my face.

"Well lucky for you, my shift ends in about ten minutes...if you're willing to wait."

"Do your stuff, and I'll wait out front." With a nod of his head, he strolled back out, and only then did I notice that every single person in the diner had been watching us. At seeing me, most quickly turned away as if busy. I belatedly realized that a lot of them had seen me all over Wilder. And then I'd just done the same with Daxon.

Whoops.

I was ready for this shift to end. I had a customer waving at me, and then I'd close out the cash register for my shift, change my clothes, and leave. Wilder would have to get a raincheck for his dessert plans.

Thirty minutes later, I emerged from the diner, exhausted but excited to find Daxon leaning against the wall near the door, hands deep in the pockets of his jacket, and with the breeze blowing through his hair, he was the epitome of the poster image of James Dean. All that was missing was a cigarette hanging out from the corner of his mouth.

"So where is this gorgeous view you promised me?" I asked, reaching his side.

His arm slid around my waist, and he looped me to swing around so we were face to face, both of us pressed together. My breath caught in my chest, my palms flat against his rock-hard chest.

"Everyone in there watches your every move."

I glanced back through the glass door to where I noticed a woman staring our way. She quickly jerked her attention away when she spotted me looking.

"Yeah, it seems that way. I guess they have nothing exciting going on in their lives." I didn't want to bring up the whole bet thing or any comparison between what I had with the alphas and what Arcadia did. I wanted nothing to do with her. "Come on, let's get out of here, I'm tired of being watched."

"Agreed." But before he let me go, his mouth found mine and he kissed me with a slow passion, one that was all lips and no tongue, where he sucked on my lips. His strong fingers pressed into my lower back with the urgency to do so much more with him. "I love the way you taste."

I buzzed from my head down to my toes at his words.

With a final quick peck on my lips, he guided me to join him as he took my hand into his, and we headed down the road. I took a quick side-glance into the diner, where I could have sworn every single eye was on us.

"You kissed me so they would all look, didn't you?"

"It worked, right? The people in this town are so predictable." He held me close, and I didn't miss the patronizing tone in his voice.

His arm held me tight as we strolled down the slight slope the sidewalk followed. "I haven't seen any cliffs near town," I admitted.

"That's why we're riding there. We're just going to pick up my bike from the shop."

"Oh." A light trepidation wormed up my spine. "I've never been on a motorcycle before."

"My girl's a Ducati, and she'll purr between your legs, babe. All you need to do is wrap yourself around me and hold on. I'll do the rest."

"As long as you promise I won't fall off, I'm game."

"Promise," he said with a chuckle before giving me a quick look, the glow of the descending sun blinking in his eyes.

Upon our arrival at the shop, a loud crash boomed. It took me moments to make out the shadows inside the garage, spotting North, the large guy who worked there, stumbling backward. I'd met him after arriving in Amarok, and he looked just as pissed and growly then as he did now. As before, he wore grease streaked grey over-alls, his white tee underneath just as filthy. Shaggy brown hair lined with grey hair feathered around his face, making him look more like a wild man who'd just found civilization.

"Stay here," Daxon said, pushing me to stand just outside the open roller doors. He then proceeded to march inside.

"Everything all right, North?" he asked, his shoulders broad and unafraid.

North murmured something I couldn't decipher, then

he lurched forward, vanishing behind a car sitting partially up on the hoist.

All I could see were two pairs of legs moving about on the other side of the car, and growls echoed against the walls. What the hell was going on?

I moved to stand to the side of the entrance, hoping for a better view, when North came teetering out, a heavy snarl in his throat. And when his head snapped in my direction, piercing yellow eyes stared at me...eyes that weren't human but wolf.

Daxon was at his side in seconds, wrenched an arm around his throat and dragged him backward. "It's for your own good, buddy, now don't fight me." He dragged the man into the main office where I lost sight of them. But I could hear the crashing sound of things falling over and snarls echoing out to where I stood. There were a few more bangs, and then it fell silent.

I chewed on a fingernail, peering in closer, not that I could see anything, but I was worried. "Daxon, everything all right?" I called out.

Fear skittered down my back, and I could only hazard a guess that somehow North had lost control of his wolf. I'd seen it happen once before back in Alistair's pack, when a new young member lost control under the full moon. It shouldn't have, but I'd heard others say it took a while to tame your wolf. Except North looked like he might be in his sixties, so it couldn't be that.

When no response came, I glanced behind me to the empty street, where the nearby stores were shut. Sweat slicked my palms, and I rubbed them down my pants. "Daxon?"

A twinge of pain rose through my chest, reminding me of the ache I felt the other night by the river. Except that was just a dream, nothing else. Even my research showed nothing.

Suddenly, Daxon emerged from the office and shut the door behind him. He was dusting off his hands. I could see there were three tears down the front of his jeans, with a bit of blood tainting the fabric.

"What the hell just happened with North? Are you okay?"

The corner of his mouth tugged upward in a smoking hot smirk. "Nothing to fear. North is a Fenrir wolf. Not many of them around, and well, he sometimes has a problem in the week of the full moon."

Wilder had told me that there were four wolf shifter breeds in the world, so I knew this, but I was still mesmerized listening to Daxon.

"I still can't believe I've never heard of them," I answered.

Daxon moved into the darker shadows of the garage, and in moments, he was rolling out a motorbike, black as the night... The thing was sleek and beautiful. It glinted in the light, and I watched him bring the bike outside the shop and park it in the driveway.

"The thing about Fenrirs is that their origins come from the berserkers, their heritage from the Vikings. They are aggressive and cunning bastards, but don't fully transform, just their eyes. Their animal dominates them more than the human side, and sometimes, the full moon will influence them and transform them without their control. Luckily, we were here just in time. We've got a

holding cell in the back, seeing that his animal side dominates when he changes, and well, he didn't quite make it
there in time."

"That sounds scary."

He turned back to the garage, and using a thick chain
at the side of the entrance, he started hauling on it,
bringing down the metal garage door.

"So North will be okay?"

Daxon shut the shop, locking up the roller door, and
came back to me. "I'll let him out in the morning and
he'll be fine." He handed me one of the helmets hanging
off the side of the bike.

He threw a leg over the bike, kicked back the parking
lever, and tapped the seat behind him. My stomach fluttered, as I couldn't wait to go for a ride, maybe get out of
town, and with Daxon...well, I felt completely safe.

With my helmet on and secured, I placed a hand on
his shoulder and climbed onto the bike behind him. The
spot didn't offer much space, and it forced me to be plas-
tered to him.

"Wrap yourself around me. Let me feel the heat of
your gorgeous pussy."

Well, all right then.

My legs straddled around his ass, and I pressed up
against him, my arms coiled around his middle. He
placed his hand on mine, his touch fiery hot.

Then he started the bike, and the motor roared to life.
It hummed and vibrated beneath me like a living beast.

We started rolling down the driveway. Once on the
road, he accelerated, and we really took off. I lurched
backward from the momentum, and I frantically tight-

ened my grasp around his body, pushing myself even closer to him. My heart hammered in my chest at how fast we moved, how the wind beat against us, how the world was a beautiful blur.

There was no pause through the town, just us speeding with the grunt of the motorbike in our wake.

Daxon took the corners smoothly, racing us up the slope that led out of town, and he only came to a halt at the T-intersection at the main road. The same place I had crashed my car, and I couldn't fathom how long ago that felt, how much had changed since I stumbled into this town blindly.

The spot reminded me that we'd just been at the shop and I hadn't even bothered to look for my car or ask about it.

Things really had changed.

"You okay?" he called out, turning his head toward me, lifting his visor.

"This is amazing," I responded, to which he laughed.

"Good. Now hold on."

We started moving again, and this time, the speed we drove left me slightly terrified. I held him with a death grip while taking in the scenery. The stunning greenery around us, the thick woods on either side, the sun bleeding through the gaps, giving everything an eerie glow. Absolutely gorgeous.

When we finally came out into a clearing, I glanced over to where the mountain range had my mouth dropping open with awe, and in the afternoon sky, the pale ghostly moon hung, waiting to steal away daylight.

We rode faster, and I held on tighter, loving this

escape from reality more than Daxon would ever imagine. To be taken out and treated this way was doing something to me, as Alistair rarely took me outside the house, let alone anything special like this.

Why was I even thinking about him?

My life was changing for the better, if only I could get to the stage where I could put the past behind me for good.

When we finally turned off the main road, the ground grew bumpy, and we slowed down. It didn't take long for us to come out onto a clearing that led to a gorgeous cliff that dropped off into the abyss in the distance. The path between the edge and us had been impassable with a bike, so Daxon parked near a tree, and we climbed off.

My legs wobbled, and it almost felt like I was walking on air. Daxon unzipped his leather jacket and laid it over the bike's seat. When I glanced out over the horizon, where the sun shone brightly, I sighed. The afternoon shadows lengthened over the land, and it was magnificent.

In that moment, an unexpected sting flared from deep in my chest, bringing with it a panic that something was wrong with me. My heart pounded like a desperate drum leading up to a tragic ending.

I couldn't breathe suddenly as I kept picturing losing control, passing out.

Gravel crunched behind me, and Daxon pressed against my back. "You okay? What's going on?" His hands gripped my waist and twisted me around to face him.

A whimper came from my mouth when I tried to speak, and a frighting expression flared over his face.

"Talk to me, what's going on?"

But my response was stolen by the heavy crunch of tires on gravel from the direction we'd arrived. We both twisted around to find a black Mercedes pulling up at least twenty feet from the Ducati.

Who was that?

The air suddenly thickened, and a fiery heat came from Daxon, a threatening growl rising from him at the newcomers.

"Stay behind me," he ordered as he stepped in front of me. The tone of his voice told me he believed the person pulling up wasn't a friend, but it could just be humans wanting to see the view, right?

The bang of a car door grabbed my attention, followed by several more, and I looked out past Daxon to four huge men coming toward us.

Nope, this was not a happy family coming for the view, not with the way they stared at us with a dark intensity.

My skin crawled, and my throat tightened.

"You've taken the wrong turn," Daxon mocked them, his voice loud and deep, his shoulders squared. I noticed he was gripping a blade behind his back. Where did he get that from?

"Get the fuck out of our way," the man with a bald head barked, his chest sticking out. Like the rest of his crew, he was rippling with muscles.

My thoughts flew to Sterling's recent arrival, but none of these men looked familiar to me.

The shortest one at the back started twitching, then

two others followed suit, their bodies stretching, elongating, and I gasped at the sight.

I backed away as my insides crumbled at the sight of the shifters transforming.

They were wolves.

Coming for us...for me.

All doubt dissolved about these men being anything but danger.

They definitely belonged to Alistair.

Fear pounded into me. Obviously, there was no safety in Amarok from that monster. Not anymore, if more of these men were coming for me.

The ache in my chest returned, coming at me in waves, and I rubbed the pain with my fist, dark thoughts flooding my head as I stared at the transformation happening in front of me. Ones where I'd be dragged back to Alistair, where he'd torture me for the rest of my life. Anger burst forward, and I curled my hands into fists because I'd throw myself off the cliff before I'd ever return to him. Death was a welcome friend compared to being with him.

"They're here from my ex," I cried, my throat raspy.

"Don't be scared," Daxon said casually.

"There's four of them," I murmured, staring at the three men now rising from the ground in their wolf form. All of them wore gray fur, while only Mr. Baldy remained in his human form to approach us.

"You're going to die today, my friend," he warned Daxon. "How that goes down depends on you. Put up a fight, and it will hurt. Give up now, and we'll make it fast."

Daxon laughed. "Am I supposed to be scared?" he purred.

"It's four against one."

"Well, *friend*. Your first mistake was daring to follow us here. Your second was underestimating me. My face is going to be the last thing you remember."

I blinked and tried to swallow, but my body wasn't listening. Between the growing pain spearing through my body and the predators approaching, I felt trapped.

My ears rang with each thumping heartbeat.

Then in a flash, chaos broke out so fast, it ripped away my world. It all happened too quick. A cry broke from my lips as the three wolves viciously attacked Daxon. They all hit the ground in a great heap, and all I saw were fur and teeth, their terrifying growls piercing the earlier silence.

The bald man charged at me. Fire singed my insides as I staggered backward, searching the ground frantically for a weapon, but what chance did I stand? So I did the only thing possible... I turned and ran.

Suddenly, a huge weight collided with my back, and next thing I knew, I flew face first to the ground. The ugly feelings surfacing inside me brought back all the times Alistair had punished me in just this position. I had to push back the fear...and the vomit, threatening to erupt.

"He misses you," the man muttered, his putrid breath on the back of my head. "And you know what he said? We can bring you back in any state, as long as you are still fucking alive." He reached down and shoved me onto my back. "I've always wanted to fuck an alpha's bitch."

A chill wrapped around me. "Don't touch me," I cried

back, and a snarl unleashed from deep inside me, leaving me shaking.

He laughed, but really, could I expect anything less from someone willing to work for Alistair?

"Fuck you!" I said, turning my head to spit in his face.

The flat of his hand connected with the side of my face so fast, I only saw stars.

With it, a crack of electricity pricked my skin as I moaned and shoved against him to escape.

"Have you been spreading your legs for that wolf, whore?"

"Get off me!" I hurled my fists into his face, thrust my body, and kicked. Desperation owned me, and I didn't hear the rest of what he said. Between him and my body shaking violently, I just needed air.

I lashed out and scratched the side of his face, my fingernails tearing through skin. His eyes widened, his twisted expression horrified.

"You fucking bitch." He got to his feet, snatched me by my hair, and wrenched me to my knees.

I lurched after him, my scalp screaming with pain, and without thought, I threw my fist directly at his groin, putting all my weight behind my punch.

He squealed, his grip softening, and I fell backward. I scrambled to my feet, the feral battle with Daxon and the wolves calling to me. My head felt fuzzy all of a sudden, and a thunderous gasp rolled from my lips as my legs gave out from under me. I clutched the grass, swaying as the pain slashed over my chest, swallowing me. My body suddenly jerked, my back arching, a loud crack of bones sounding.

Fear throttled me.

I shook ferociously as an inferno seized my body, and a half-scream, half-howl tore past my throat.

I drowned in terror as my limbs jerked just the same, extending, snapping, my skin popping as it split open, replaced by white fur that burst over my body. My clothes shredded around me, and I screamed from the acid-like pain. My cries soon morphed into a guttural growl that didn't sound like me, but it definitely had come from me.

Stumbling around on all fours, the pain suddenly faded. I lifted my head, and the world appeared different, the colors sharper, shadows crisp, and my nose was flooded with powerful smells. Perspiration, muskiness, and blood. Beyond that lay the pines and fresh earth, but also a wave of trepidation. Birds chirped from so far away, yet I heard them perfectly.

"How the fuck?!" the bald man blurted, staring down at me incredulously. And it took me seconds to work out that he was talking about me. I glanced down, and instead of my hands on the ground, I found large silvery paws and white fur all the way up my legs.

I wobbled as shock poured over me.

I was a wolf. I'd done it. About fucking time!

The crunch of foliage had me jerking my head up just as Daxon, still in human form and covered in blood, raced up behind Mr. Baldy.

A strange empty look bled into Daxon's gaze, one of death as though he might be the Grim Reaper coming for souls. He gripped a long butcher's knife and moved swiftly. Behind him, the three wolves staggered off the ground, also covered in blood. It amazed me how much damage Daxon had done with it being three against one.

His gaze lifted to mine for a split second, his mouth parting in what looked like surprise as he knew it was me in wolf form.

In a heartbeat, Daxon swung the weapon at the man's back, just as the man snapped around, clearly sensing his approach.

The blade swished through the air, and Daxon jammed it right into the guy's chest so fiercely, it went all the way through his body and came out the other end.

I cringed on the inside at how painful it looked.

"I fucking told you I'd be the last thing you'd see," Daxon snarled, his anger terrifying.

The man collapsed, gurgling his last response. Blood spilled out from the corners of his mouth, his body convulsing.

Movement behind Daxon caught my attention. The three wolves were up and stalking toward him.

Rage ignited in my chest and something took over me, electricity zipping down my spine. Blind fury burned in my veins at them hurting what was mine. Next thing I knew, I burst forward, my teeth gnashing, their death the only thing on my mind.

Daxon

RUNE ZIPPED RIGHT PAST ME, her fur white as snow, her paws streaked with silver. She was spectacular. My gorgeous girl had finally found her wolf. She'd transformed, and I couldn't have been prouder of her. I kicked the dead asshole in the ribs for making me miss her special moment.

My gorgeous girl lunged at the three bastards sneaking up on me, crashing into one wolf so powerfully, he hit the ground with a whimpering sound. She moved like the wind, whipping from one to the other, faster than I'd seen any wolf move, let alone a brand-new one.

Her attack was precise and cruel. She latched onto one of the wolf's throat and ripped out his jugular without hesitation or struggle. I couldn't possibly adore her more as blood splashed across the white on her face.

When another gray wolf charged for her from the rear, I lunged toward him and snatched him by the back of his scruff with both hands, shaking the fuck out of him. "Don't worry, you'll get your chance to die. My little wolf girl is hungry for blood today."

Watching her was extraordinary, but the longer she fought, the more I noticed something odd. Everywhere her paws struck, she left behind a silvery footprint, one that floated on the breeze like dust seconds afterward.

That was peculiar and something I'd never seen before. And well, I'd seen my fair share of fucked up shit, but that left me speechless.

The idiot in my grasp kept twisting his head towards me, teeth snapping at me, or at least trying to reach me. Seeing how much fun Rune was having, I released the beast. He'd barely gained his balance before Rune lunged at him, her teeth ripping into his side, tearing flesh away. His cries were music to my ears, her fierceness rather arousing.

My cock twitched at the way she so ruthlessly tore into the wolf's underbelly, and what made the image a lot more perfect was the floating of silver particles from her footprints. The scene took on a very different macabre feel to have the splash of blood and sparkle of silver tangled together. Who the hell knew what the silver marking meant, but with it being Rune, it was beautiful.

These wolves stood no chance against her. I never imagined she'd be so powerful, so fucking incredibly vicious.

When she finally came to rest, her chest pumping for oxygen, she stared at her handiwork, at how artfully she'd streaked the earth with their blood.

I'd never been more attracted to anyone as I was at this very moment.

"You've done spectacularly." I laid a hand on her back, her body scorching hot under my palm.

She lifted her head, looking at me with huge silvery blue eyes, and behind them, lay my girl. She whimpered, and I shook my head. "No, don't be ashamed. This is what you were born to do, and you are fucking gorgeous."

Energy buzzed up my arms as her body trembled, and I watched the way her body quivered and stretched, the fur retreating into her body. My heart beat harder at watching something so personal, it gave me shivers. Her honeyed and sexy scent drove me mad, and my muscles bunched as she collapsed onto the ground in her human form.

She was naked, her body smeared in blood, and my cock thickened at the sight. There was nothing more alluring than the blend of blood and sex.

I bent down and scooped her into my arms. She glanced up at me, her eyes still holding onto her wildness, and my heart stuttered. My insides twisted at the craving that roared within me.

"You are everything to me," I said. "And I'm going to fuck you now."

She pulled herself to meet my face, wrapped her hands behind my neck, and kissed me with approval, with demand, with urgency.

*M*y mind twisted with so many emotions, my body was shaking from adrenaline...I didn't know where to focus.

I'd turned into a wolf!

I. Had. Turned. Into. A. Wolf.

I wanted to scream, but exhaustion rattled me, and instead, I found myself drawn to Daxon. The way he watched me fight and transform had me buzzing, seeing the acceptance in his eyes. He looked proud at the way I'd killed those men. Not that I was a killer... I'd never been one, but I'd managed to take out three powerful wolves with such ease that it scared me a bit. I had no idea where the transformation had come from, but the ravenous hunger of my wolf wasn't what I'd expected.

Being in Daxon's arms covered me in warmth and chased away the fear.

So I kissed him harder, desperate for him, wanting to inhale his breath into me because I didn't want to face what I'd just done. I couldn't deal with that, not yet anyway. Besides, with the way his fingers dug into my back, his kiss so aggressive, I knew without doubt that he was all about the messed up and broken side of me. And I clung onto that with every piece of my aching soul.

"Please, Daxon," I begged, my throat sounding ragged. The taste of blood on the back of my tongue seemed to only fuel my arousal, my hunger. "Make me feel something other than fear."

He carried me across the grounds, stepping over the bodies, and said, "There is nothing to be afraid of. What you did was a miracle. It's unheard of for a wolf to transform on her own after her fated mate suppressed her wolf. You're special. I knew you were and maybe a lot more like me than either of us ever realized."

I wasn't sure how to respond. All I knew was that my mind was filled with a savage hunger to hunt, to kill...and to fuck. In my defense, out of those three desires, I chose the one that had already offered itself to me, a temptation I couldn't resist.

When we reached the black Mercedes, he placed a flat hand against the hood, then laid me down on my back. The warmth of the motor was comforting against my back, and Daxon followed, covering me with his body, his mouth claiming mine. His tongue swept down my jaw, across my collarbone, and found my pebbled nipple, which he hungrily took into his mouth.

I arched at the way he tugged on them with his mouth and fingers. I breathed faster as I wriggled beneath him, urgency climbing through me, just as my wolf had done earlier.

I gripped the fabric of his shirt, tugging it upward to take it off him.

He laughed at me and reared back to stand up. "Let me get that for you." Even with his shirt shredded, he took his time unbuttoning, teasing me. "Spread your legs for me. Show me how wet you are."

He reached down and nudged at my knees, which I drew up and spread wide, offering him all of me, putting myself on display. I no longer felt shy, quite the opposite. With so much adrenaline still coursing through my veins, blushing was the last thing on my mind, as my heart still beat frantically from the fight. I'd never imagined how unbelievably satisfying it would be, and finally, I understood why wolves loved to hunt and fight. It was ingrained in us, made us who we were at the core.

Licking his lips, Daxon unbuckled his belt and dropped his pants. Of course he was commando underneath. I doubted he ever wore underwear.

My hand shook as I reached out for him, while he took in the perfect view he had of my body.

"You're so beautiful and wet for me, baby."

With one hand, he grasped his thick cock and palmed at it several times, while his other hand found the apex between my legs. He pressed two fingers into my soaking opening, sliding them in easily. "I love the sound of your pussy sucking on me."

He hissed his own pleasure, while I moaned, and when he leaned down over me, my back bowed against the hood as I tried to push my mouth hard to his.

For a moment, I wondered if I might go insane with

need at how much my body trembled for his touch, but the more he took his time, the more desperate I felt.

"Daxon," I moaned.

He snarled under his breath, kissing me with savagery, pulling me a little closer to him. When he pushed the tip of his cock into me, I purred beneath him. "Is that what you've wanted?" he asked.

"Yes. I want it all," I groaned.

With one hand pressed to the car's hood over my shoulder, he slid his other hand down my side and grabbed my ass. He scooped my ass upward, giving him the perfect position.

"Today, you've somehow become so much more than I'd ever dreamed about. You're perfect, my mate. I'm going to make you mine." His tip pushed into me, stretching me open.

I could barely make sense of his words with my focus centered on the way he forced himself into me. I growled a bit each time he withdrew to slowly edge deeper.

His eyes seemed to glow. "Your flawless cunt is so tight." And with those words, he thrust into me all the way, merging our bodies as one. "You're all mine."

I cried out, gripping his strong shoulders as he pumped into me several more times, each harder than the last. My whole body shifted in rhythm with him rocking into me, my legs closing around his hips.

"Good girl," he murmured heavily in my ear, his hands now gripping my hips, holding me exactly where he needed me. He left a trail of soft kisses along the curve of my neck, his breaths speeding up while relentlessly fucking me with his rock-hard cock.

We moved in rhythm, him riding me. I moaned for him to take all of me, to help me forget what I'd done, where we were, or that around us lay bodies I'd slayed.

He growled my name as he plunged into me, my body growing tighter, my screams louder. He greedily kissed me, and the buildup inside me rushed forward like a storm.

"I'll always give you what you want, Rune," he whispered heavily, never ceasing his thrusting, while my desperation to release clawed at my insides, my wolf pushing forward, sensing we were so close now.

She groaned beneath my breastbone, and I felt her calling to Daxon's wolf, his wolf growling in response. Like animals, we fucked hard. I held onto him, losing myself to a pleasure so intense, I forgot everything else.

He watched me the whole time, sliding his cock in and out of me, the friction igniting our blaze. He pushed and pushed me, and when I finally tumbled over the edge, my whole body convulsed.

"Daxon," I cried out, my back arching, my head tilting back, my hands clawing at his arms. Every inch of me clenched around him.

"Fuck, I love you so much."

His words were like honey, coming at the right moment, and I wanted to react, needed to, but I was too far gone, floating on pleasure, on a heart-spinning orgasm. But he'd said the love word, and I wanted to cry at hearing someone say that to me.

Before I could even try to say anything as I writhed and screamed, his mouth was on my left shoulder, peppering me with kisses. Then a biting sharpness sunk into my flesh.

I screamed from the sudden pain while still in the throes of climaxing. He had me pinned beneath him, suddenly releasing in me, pulsing. A snarl rolled from his throat as he remained attached to my shoulder, licking at the blood he'd drawn.

At the mark he'd left me.

And even while still coming down from my high, his earlier words came to me.

I'm going to make you mine.

That was exactly what he'd done. He'd marked me as his own.

Fuck. I moaned, caught in the overbearing heat from our bodies and how magical the moment felt, yet torn at the same time at the fact that he'd bitten me. After a few moments, the truth crashed into me. His hot breath suddenly grazed my ear.

"You're everything to me," he whispered, and suddenly, I was lost to his earlier comment.

I love you.

My heart melted, and suddenly, all the earlier worries melted away. I wanted nothing to ruin this perfect moment. He pulled out of me and rolled onto the side of the hood alongside me, drawing me into his arms. He looked into my eyes. "You have no idea how perfect you are."

I smiled, my chest beaming, and I leaned my head against his chest, listening to his pounding heart. There had been so many times that I'd waited for Alistair to want me the way Daxon did, to whisper those words in my ears. I blinked back tears at the joy I never expected.

Except for some reason, something at the back of my mind kept nagging me, refusing to leave me alone. My heart drummed, and I tried to push it away when it came flooding to the forefront of my mind.

"Oh shit!"

"*F*uck, what time is it?" I asked, struggling to come out of my orgasm haze.

Daxon lazily got off the hood of the car and picked up his phone from his pants on the ground. "Five forty-five," he drawled.

My stomach suddenly cramped up. "Hell. I'm going to be late! We have to get back!" I slid off the Mercedes, my muscles aching deliciously. I was butt naked, and my clothes had been ripped in my shift. I didn't really want to roll back into town with my boobs hanging out.

"Here, gorgeous," Daxon said, handing me his leather jacket that he'd taken off before everything went crazy. Thank goodness.

I slipped it on and zipped it up. It fell to mid-thigh and covered my butt, but I still looked hesitantly at his bike, not really jazzed about riding naked on that thing.

"We'll borrow the Mercedes. I don't think that any of these gentlemen will mind," Daxon said with a dark snicker. "I'll come back for the bike later."

It felt a bit creepy to drive their car, but beggars couldn't be choosers and all of that.

I pushed Daxon towards the driver's seat. "Come on, we have to hurry," I said in a raspy voice. My throat was done with all the screaming I'd just done. Totally worth it though.

Daxon didn't seem to be in a hurry to go anywhere. His gaze slid down my body, and flames sprung to life in their depths. I had to admit I thought about going for round two for a hot minute, but I held myself back because I was an adult, thank you very much.

I dove into the passenger seat before he could lure me with his wicked ways. I watched as he strolled over to the dead bald guy that had been driving and grabbed the car keys from the man's pocket. Daxon pushed the knife further into the man's chest for good measure and shot me a smile that was all bad boy. Not for the first time, I wondered how it was possible for both him and Wilder to exist in one town. They were easily the hottest guys I'd ever seen in my entire life.

Wilder.

My heart squeezed when I thought of him. I rubbed at the mark Daxon had left on my shoulder. It was aching a bit, not healing as fast as everything else seemed to now. I wanted it to heal as fast as everything else seemed to be lately.

Daxon finally turned the car on, and we sped towards the old mansion on the outskirts of town where Miyu's ceremony was taking place. Evidently, it was where most of the major town events happened, both for the Bitten and the Lycan packs.

We both were quiet during the drive, lost in our thoughts. I'd found some baby wipes in the glove box, and I'd wiped all the blood off my visible skin. I'd luckily be able to take a shower at the venue.

Daxon kept shooting me meaningful looks like he wanted to say something, but I didn't encourage him by asking him what he was thinking. I felt...fragile after what had just happened. Like I'd just been cut open and my ugly insides were now visible to him and the rest of the world.

He'd tried to give me a mating bite.

Just thinking about it made the wound on my shoulder throb even more. I didn't know what I thought about that. I was a little bit angry because we hadn't really discussed it. But I was also a little bit angry because what was he doing wanting to mate with someone like me? Not that I thought it was really possible, but there wasn't anything he could do that could replace the bond that I would have had with Alistair. Even rejected, a true mate sat there in your veins, calling for you, even when all you wanted to do was forget. I wouldn't want Daxon to be secondary in any way, but what could I do?

A deep bitterness wove its way through my heart when I thought about how unfair everything was. It was a life-changing realization to acknowledge that if I could pick him or Wilder as my true mate, I would. I'd found two men who somehow completed me. Our souls matched, even with as different as the two of them were, it felt like they had been put on the earth for me.

How cruel was it that the moon goddess had

prevented me from ever being able to complete the promise of what could be with them?

And then of course there was the fact that there were two of them. And they hated each other. It was all a mess.

We pulled around a half-circle drive in front of a white mansion that reminded me of the giant estate houses in Savannah or Charleston I'd seen pictures of in books. It looked like it had been plucked right out of the pages of *Gone with the Wind* and was a little bit out of place in this town. But Amarok was always full of surprises, I guessed. The library was proof of that.

Daxon looked at me and opened his mouth, and I bolted out of the car like a coward. I didn't want to hear what he had to say. I didn't want to hear him tell me that he loved me again or anything else that would just make all of this worse.

Daxon

I watched as she ran inside, obviously having forgotten that she was wearing just my leather coat. I'm sure that would give anyone who saw her some gossip to talk about during the ceremony, even though the jacket covered all the important parts.

These things were always dreadfully boring though, so it would at least liven things up. Not that Rune needed more gossip about her.

Fuck. My thoughts were all over the place. And they all revolved around her. Wondering what she was thinking, what she was feeling. Did she feel this all-encompassing madness for me that I felt for her?

I doubted it.

Actually, I was sure she didn't feel it.

Because watching her walk away felt like a piece of me was dying, and judging by how fast she was running, there was no dying happening on her end.

The bond hadn't taken. I'd heard of that happening, but never in this kind of situation. I'd heard of it not working because the one giving the bite didn't have deep enough emotions to complete the magic necessary for the bond.

That wasn't what had happened here. Rune was somehow blocking the magic of the bond. And it didn't have anything to do with the fact that she had a true mate out there. A wolf could have a true mate bond, and a mate bond. Miyu's parents were proof of that. If you couldn't have both, her father would have been shit out of luck when he met her mother. As much as it burned at my gut to know that she would have a true mate bond that would always trump my mate bond, until I killed him of course, I had accepted it, desperate to get whatever I could get from her.

But then she hadn't accepted the fucking thing. I felt shattered, desperate to make her feel what I was feeling so that I could try again. I would make her fall in love with me. I would make it so that she couldn't live without me. I would be everything she'd ever needed. I would make her obsessed with me.

She'd never get away.

Decision made, I got out of the car, feeling much

more cheerful about everything. I walked into the mansion, nodding at the random townspeople I passed. Miyu and Rae were both Bitten, but they were popular enough that there were lots of members of Wilder's pack here as well. He'd unfortunately be here too.

Speak of the bastard. Wilder was leaning against a wall, talking to some of his pack while he sipped champagne from a fancy flute glass. He was all decked out in a fitted tux. Luckily, my tux was waiting in the groom's quarters somewhere here, since it was my job to officiate the damn thing as their alpha. Just beyond Wilder, I could see Arcadia staring desperately at him. I slipped up the stairs before she could see me. That was one way to ruin everything quickly. I'd probably snap and kill the bitch, and then the party would be ruined.

Pity.

I whistled as I walked up the stairs to get ready to do this thing. Everything was going to work out. I'd make sure of it.

Rune

"ARE YOU READY?" I asked softly, buttoning up what seemed like the millionth button on the back of Miyu's dress.

"I think so," she squealed as we both admired her in the floor length mirror in front of us. She was a vision in her long dark, red dress that actually went perfectly with her red hair.

Red was usually the color a shifter got married in. It

was a symbol of the shifter spirit and vitality and the forever nature of the promise she would be making today. She looked amazing in it.

The dress was sleeveless with a sweetheart neckline. It hugged every inch of her curvy body until it flared out at the bottom. A red lace overlay covered the red silk material that made up the first layer of the dress. I was obsessed with everything about it. Miyu's hair was done up in an elaborate updo with pieces that framed her heart-shaped face. Her eye makeup was simple with long fake lashes to make her eyes pop, and she had finished the look off with a dark red lipstick.

She was perfection.

"You look amazing," I told her, smoothing my dove grey dress down, anxious for everything to be perfect for my best friend.

She gave me her signature blinding smile and was about to say something when her mother popped her head in. "It's time," she announced, her gaze soft on her daughter.

Miyu squealed again before squeezing my hand and then marching towards the door. "Let's do this thing," she yelled, holding her fist up in a mock war cry. The other girls and I giggled as we watched her walk out before we followed.

The ceremony was taking place in the backyard of the mansion. An elaborate arch had been created that was covered with roses. Lanterns provided soft lighting for the event. Black chairs were set up in rows, and vases of roses were everywhere.

A violin started playing, and Miyu's father, a distinguished-looking man with a friendly face held out his arm for her to take. The rest of us got ready to go before her. Looking at the other girls, Miyu had fulfilled her promise to make us look good for the ceremony. We all looked banging. Eliza, a sweet girl who'd known Miyu since they were girls, shot me a smile and set off. Two more girls went...and then it was my turn.

I took a deep breath and then started to walk down the dramatic staircase that led down to the garden. All the guests were staring up at us while we walked down, and all the attention was a bit unnerving. I tried to keep a smile on my face, even as my nerves danced around in my stomach.

And then, I saw them. Daxon was standing at the end of the aisle, dressed in a perfectly fitted black tux that had my insides going insane. His blond hair was swept artfully across his face, and those gold eyes of his were devouring me as I tried to walk down the stairs without falling. And just a few feet away from him...was Wilder. He looked every inch the dreamy bad boy standing there in his grey tux that was just a shade darker than the dress the girls were wearing. Wilder was part of Rae's line, a sign of respect since he was the other leader in the town. His emerald eyes stared at me just as intensely as Daxon's were, and my skin felt like it was on fire from the combined force of both of their gazes. My heart wanted them. My soul wanted them.

Everything was a blur after that. I somehow made it to the front where I was supposed to stand, unaware of anything but them. Miyu and her father made it to the arch, and Daxon mercifully dragged his attention away from me and then proceeded to start the ceremony. It was beautiful and heartfelt and made my soul long for my own happy ending as I watched Miyu and Rae make their vows and share their kiss. Their bites would take place privately tonight, away from prying eyes.

Speaking of bites... Wilder's gaze was locked onto my shoulder, where I realized that some of Daxon's bite was peaking out. He looked...furious.

I touched it self-consciously.

A loud cheer filled the air as Rae and Miyu kissed. They set off down the aisle hand in hand, and the rest of the mating party followed behind them. I could feel Daxon and Wilder's gazes burning holes in my back though.

I chatted with the girls distractedly as we waited to go into the ballroom, where the reception was taking place. One by one, we were announced, and then we stepped to the side while Miyu and Rae started their first dance.

Wilder appeared next to me, his hand stroking down my skin, thanks to the nonexistent back of my dress.

"You're the most stunning creature I've ever seen," he whispered, and I shot him a shaky smile. This was the first time I'd been really dressed up since coming to this town, and even I could admit I looked good with my hair in soft waves down my back, wearing the perfectly fitted fancy dress. Goosebumps stretched out on my skin as his fingers began to dance back up my spine.

"Anything you want to tell me?" he asked suddenly.

And I knew he was talking about the mark that was thankfully now covered.

"I can sense the bond didn't work, but..." he began.

"It didn't work?" I asked, confused.

Before I could ask any more, Daxon appeared on the other side of me, smiling prettily with that perfect grin of his.

My mouth opened and then closed as the music changed. The bridal party was supposed to join Miyu and Rae out on the floor. But as Ben Harper's "Forever" began to play, Daxon and Wilder both held their hands out to me, asking me to pick one of them to take out with me on the floor. Confidence in their gazes like they had no doubt I would pick them.

I froze, my gaze flicking between the two of them. Their smiles faded as I took a step backwards, panic shooting through my heart.

I couldn't pick just one, I couldn't do it.

It suddenly felt like it was a thousand degrees in there, like I was going to pass out from the heat.

I turned without a word and stumbled away. I heard Wilder shout something after me, but I ignored him, desperate to get away.

I ran back out into the maze of hallways that made up the mansion, needing to get some fresh air before I passed out. Looking back, I didn't see either of them following me, and I breathed out a sigh of relief as I made it back out to where the ceremony had just been held and took huge gulps of the cool night air. I absentmindedly admired how the courtyard looked with the fairy lights strewn all around, all the while thinking of what I was going to do about the very real feelings I had for Wilder *and* Daxon.

I was about to go back inside when it happened.

"Hello, little moon," a very familiar voice silkily spoke in my ear.

I turned my head and stared into the face of the creature who had ruined my life.

"Alistair," I breathed, grief slicing through my body.

I guessed I wasn't going to have to worry about choosing between Daxon and Wilder again.

He'd found me.

Continue Rune's story in Wild Girl.

ABOUT C.R. JANE

A Texas girl living in Utah now, I'm a wife, mother, lawyer, and now author. My stories have been floating around in my head for years, and it has been a relief to finally get them down on paper. I'm a huge Dallas Cowboys fan and I primarily listen to Beyonce and Taylor Swift...don't lie and say you don't too.

My love of reading started probably when I was three and with a faster than normal ability to read, I've devoured hundreds of thousands of books in my life. It only made sense that I would start to create my own worlds since I was always getting lost in others'.

I like heroines who have to grow in order to become badasses, happy endings, and swoon-worthy, devoted, (and hot) male characters. If this sounds like you, I'm pretty sure we'll be friends.

I'm so glad to have you on my team...check out the links below for ways to hang out with me and more of my books you can read!

www.crjanebooks.com

Visit my **Facebook** page to get updates.

Sign up for my **newsletter** to stay updated on new releases, find out random facts about me, and get access to different points of view from my characters.

BOOKS BY C.R. JANE

The Fated Wings Series

First Impressions

Forgotten Specters

The Fallen One (a Fated Wings Novella)

Forbidden Queens

Frightful Beginnings (a Fated Wings Short Story)

Faded Realms

Faithless Dreams

Fabled Kingdoms

Fated Wings 8

The Rock God (a Fated Wings Novella)

The Timeless Affection Series

Lamented Pasts

Lost Passions

The Pack Queen Series

Queen of the Thieves

The Sounds of Us Contemporary Series (complete series)

Remember Us This Way

Remember You This Way

Remember Me This Way

Broken Hearts Academy Series (complete duet)

Heartbreak Prince

Heartbreak Lover

Ugly Hearts Series: Enemies to Lovers

Ugly Hearts

Academy of Souls Co-write with Mila Young (complete series)

School of Broken Souls

School of Broken Hearts

School of Broken Dreams

School of Broken Wings

Fallen World Series Co-write with Mila Young (complete series)

Bound

Broken

Betrayed

Belong

Thief of Hearts Co-write with Mila Young

Siren Condemned

Siren Sacrificed

Siren Awakened

The Alpha-Hole Duet

Real Alphas Bite

Kingdom of Wolves Co-write with Mila Young

Wild Moon

Wild Heart

Wild Girl

Stupid Boys Series Co-write with Rebecca Royce

Stupid Boys

Dumb Girl

Crazy Love

Breathe Me Duet Co-write with Ivy Fox (complete)

Breathe Me

Breathe You

ABOUT MILA YOUNG

Best-selling author, Mila Young tackles everything with the zeal and bravado of the fairytale heroes she grew up reading about. She slays monsters, real and imaginary, like there's no tomorrow. By day she rocks a keyboard as a marketing extraordinaire. At night she battles with her mighty pen-sword, creating fairytale retellings, and sexy ever after tales. In her spare time, she loves pretending she's a mighty warrior, walks on the beach with her dogs, cuddling up with her cats, and devouring every fantasy tale she can get her pinkies on.

Ready to read more and more from Mila Young? www.subscribepage.com/milayoung

Join my Facebook reader group.
www.facebook.com/groups/milayoungwickedreaders

For more information...
milayoungauthor@gmail.com

BOOKS BY MILA YOUNG

Shadowlands

Shadowlands Sector, One

Shadowlands Sector, Two

Shadowlands Sector, Three

The Alpha-Hole Duet

Real Alphas Bite

Kingdom of Wolves

Wild Moon

Wild Heart

Wild Girl

Chosen Vampire Slayer

Night Kissed

Moon Kissed

Blood Kissed

Winter's Thorn

To Seduce A Fae

To Tame A Fae

To Claim A Fae

Shadow Hunters Series

Boxed Set 1

Wicked Heat Series

Wicked Heat #1

Wicked Heat #2

Wicked Heat #3

Elemental Series

Taking Breath #1

Taking Breath #2

Gods and Monsters

Apollo Is Mine

Poseidon Is Mine

Ares Is Mine

Hades Is Mine

Haven Realm Series

Hunted (Little Red Riding Hood Retelling)

Cursed (Beauty and the Beast Retelling)

Entangled (Rapunzel Retelling)

Princess of Frost (Snow Queen)

Kingdom of Wolves Co-write with C.R. Jane

Wild Moon

Passions and Protectors

Ancients and Anarchy

Subscribe to Mila Young's Newsletter to receive exclusive content, latest updates, and giveaways. Join here.